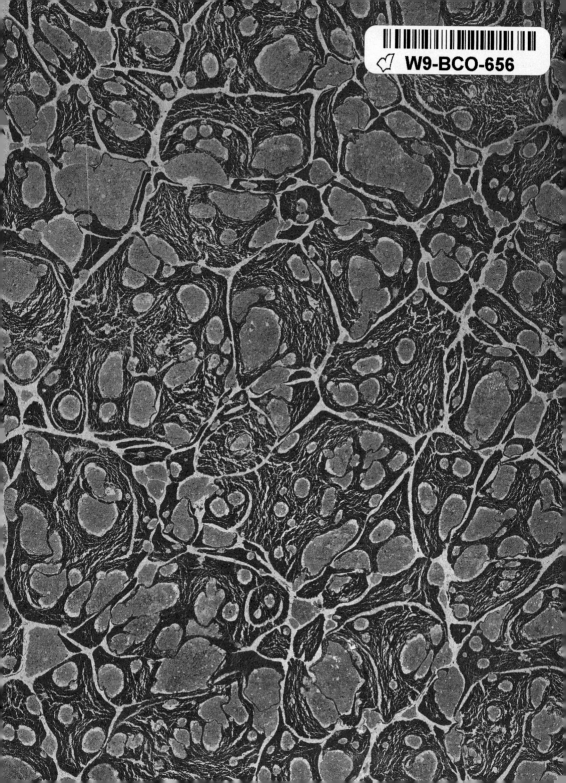

W9-BCO-656

For our sister
M. S. & J. S.

In memory of Group Captain Bill
"Dipper" Deacon and all who were made
to suffer through war.
A. D.

Marcus Sedgwick   Julian Sedgwick

VOYAGES IN THE
UNDERWORLD
OF ORPHEUS BLACK

illustrated by Alexis Deacon

WALKER
BOOKS

Right: **Harry Black's summons letter for**

a conscientious objector's tribunal.

Dated January 31, 1944.

BEFORE THIS FORM IS HANDED TO AN APPLICANT THE ADDRESS OF THE APPROPRIATE DIVISIONAL OFFICE OF THE MINISTRY OF LABOUR AND NATIONAL SERVICE AND THE DATE OF THE LAST DAY OF THE PRESCRIBED PERIOD MUST BE INSERTED IN DIRECTION (2) BELOW

NATIONAL SERVICE (ARMED FORCES) ACT, 1939

APPLICATION TO LOCAL TRIBUNAL BY A PERSON PROVISIONALLY REGISTERED IN THE REGISTER OF CONSCIENTIOUS OBJECTORS

For Official use.

Date of receipt of form. 1.31.1944

(If the form is received at a Local Office the date of receipt should be entered and the form sent immediately to the Divisional Office.)

Case No... N.W.1729 ....

Cause List :— 67

Sheet No........ 5

Line No........

Directions to Applicant :—

(1) The particulars asked for below must be given by the applicant.

(2) When completed, the application must be forwarded to the Divisional Office of the Ministry of Labour and National Service at ....

The latest day for receipt of the application at the Divisional Office is... March 1st, 1944 .....(date).

(1) Name in full. BLACK Harry Walter ....

(Surname first in BLOCK CAPITALS)

(2) Address in full.............

BORDER HOUSE, OLD FORD LANE, KNIGHTON, SHROPSHIRE.

Any statement you wish to submit in support of your application should be made below :—

I conscientiously object to being registered in the Military

Service register:-

"Greed has poisoned men's souls, has barricaded the world

with hate, has goose-stepped us into misery and bloodshed.

We have developed speed, but we have shut ourselves in.

Machinery that gives abundance has left us in want.

Our knowledge has made us cynical.

Our cleverness, hard and unkind.

We think too much and feel too little.

More than machinery we need humanity.

More than cleverness we need kindness and gentleness.

Without these qualities, life will be violent and all will be lost..."

From "The Great Dictator" by Charlie Chaplin

(Continue overleaf if necessary)

N.S.14.

[TURN OVER

NATIONAL SERVICE (ARMED FORCES) ACT, 1939.

Certificate of Registration in Register of Conscientious Objectors

D.O. NW Case No. 1729

Date 9.2.44

Holder's Name HARRY WALTER BLACK

Home Address BORDER HOUSE, OLD FORD LANE, KNIGHTON, SHROPSHIRE

Date of Birth 6.6.25.

Holder's Signature *HW Black*

This is to certify that the above person by order of the competent Tribunal is—

*Delete alternative before issue.

*(a) registered unconditionally in the Register of Conscientious Objectors.

*(b) registered conditionally in the Register of Conscientious Objectors.

(Divisional Controller, Ministry of Labour and National Service _____ N W _____ Division)

READ THIS CAREFULLY.

Care should be taken not to lose this certificate, but in the event of loss application for a duplicate should be made to the nearest Office of the Ministry of Labour and National Service.

If you change your home address or your name you must complete the space on the other side of this certificate and post it at once. A new certificate will then be sent to you.

A person who uses or lends this certificate or allows it to be used by any other person with intent to deceive, renders himself liable to heavy penalties.

N.S. 62. *43084 0/39 70*

Above: **Harry Black's conscientious objector's registration card.**

Issued February 18, 1944.

Right: **Front cover of Harry Black's notebook. December 1944**

This book belongs to Harry Black

No. 34 Fire Force, Hampstead.

If found please return, or, if not

possible, send to Sgt E the Black,

Royal Welsh Fusiliers

Failing that:

please destroy

...riors of the
...Machine.

Interior spread from
Harry Black's notebook.
December 1944

Black Out

Electricity.

Robot bombs.

The dark cave, also known as the Underworld.

Trans-cranial subsonic manipulation.

Courage and cowardice,

fear, abhorrence

and love.

The light of the sun.

I'll sing of all of these things before I am done.

I've a story to tell of Harry Black,

who went to the Underworld and how he came back;

of the love for his brother who'd pushed him away.

Of London by starlight, under attack,

of bombs falling, of people calling

   through the darkened streets,

of sirens and wayfarers, of lost souls,

of vicious women and mindless dogs.

These are the things of which I'll sing.

These, and besides them, many things more:

the persistent thrumming from deep underground,

the way that firelight flickers on faces,

and how the air vibrates after the smack of a bomb.

Of underground rivers and swarming drones,

and a pale German girl who wants to find home.

Of eyeballs and landlords and tankards of beer.

Of laughter when danger's near.

Of Harry (and his brother, Ellis) and —

What's that? What's that?

Who am I?

Ask me slowly . . .

. . . and I'll tell you.

Who am I?

I am Orpheus.

Musician, singer, poet and guide:

at your service!

Always.

You've met me before — in the streets, on the hills, at

   the edge of the milling crowd. When I stood like a

   wanderer at the cusp of your vision — that was me.

When you thought you heard singing but couldn't be sure,

   when you felt someone breathe on the back of your

   neck, and when a voice said follow, but you didn't dare.

That was me.

When something whispered inside your head, and

   implored you to listen, urged you to open your eyes,

   begged you to believe, hoped beyond hope that you

   would decide to expose your mind to something

   more; called out to you to say, Wake up!

Wake up!

Wake up!

When that happened . . .

Was that me too? Or was it you?

Perhaps it was both of us.

Perhaps we were working together, you and I,

    because we have already met.

Mine is the oldest story of all. Mine, or one very much

    like it; in which a hero with gifts beyond all measure (in

    my case the gods had taught me to sing) ventures into

    the deepest cave of greatest danger, going to face the

    ultimate foe — the one who waits on a throne in the

    dark, with a patient smile and a fingernail ticking.

Descent to the Underworld, the story so old it

    existed before there were words with which to

    tell it. To venture into the dark cave . . .

And the outcome? Triumph, or tragedy? For either can

    occur; there are no guarantees where our hero is going.

Triumph or tragedy? In my case, a little of both.

And yes, you have met me before.

My reputation rests on the power of my song;

I could still the beasts; charm birds from the trees;

    make fighting men sit down and weep.

My song could change the course of streams,

make stones rise up and dance.

Make trees lift their roots

and stride to the sea.

My reputation rests on my song,

and the fact

that I went to Hell, and back.

Orpheus, Orphée, Orfeo.

Hermes, Theseus.

Gilgamesh.

Odin.

Even Alice, who went to wrestle with the

 unconscious of her creator.

You have met me before.

And now I'll sing to you of Harry Black, disowned

 by his father, shunned by his brother, but with

 gifts beyond all measure (in his case, a skill

 with a pencil like a wizard with a wand).

The stage is dark.

Blacked out.

And as the curtain lifts, fire falls on London town ...

———————————

Boxing Day, 1944, 4:15 p.m.

Winter dusk in Kilburn, London. The world has been reduced to rubble and flame and dirty water, and the rockets and buzz bombs are falling again.

They bring death in two ways. The first, you receive some kind of warning at least. A siren, an engine growling and then cutting, a searchlight picking out chunks of shadow between the clouds. And the second, where it just hurtles at you from a clear sky, where there's no advance sound, no wailing, no time for a last thought. It simply arrives, annihilates, and only then comes all the noise and fury trailing in its wake for the survivors to hear. Then, if I'm still lucky enough to be amongst those survivors, I have to clear up what comes after.

Obliteration is our daily business, these days. *My* daily business.

I told Father I didn't want any part of it, told Ellis just the same, but one way or another, death pulls you in, and you are meshed into the machinery of war.

The strange thing is you get used to it after a hundred nights or more. You get used to anything in time, I suppose . . . or at least you think you do.

But tonight something has *changed,* as if a switch has been thrown deep inside me. And I need to try and understand what has happened—and start to do things differently.

Begin with immediate reality when you need to make sense of things, my old art teacher always said. Start with what's *bang slap in front of your damn nose* if you want to put the world into perspective.

So: the air smells of cold and smoke and burning plastic. I can hear flames crack as they devour the last of the factory we were never going to be able to save, a distant shudder as something big slams into Hackney and the ground rumbles. There are people shouting, a dog barking, and faintly—bizarrely!—someone scratching out a tune on a fiddle, a weird little melody that keeps repeating over and over, tickling away at the night air. Above me the sky is slashed by searchlights, and the antiaircraft boys are banging away at any hint of a ghost or shadow they can see now that the fog's blown clear. Yellow tracer and orange shell bursts to make a good show, lighting up the barrage balloons, littering the city with thousands more shards of hot metal.

Pointless.

But good for Father's business; good for the family's fortunes. The gunners are making the most of the clear spell, eating up the shells made by Black and Company at an appalling rate. They have some chance with the doodlebugs—they're slow enough to hit—but the new rockets are just too fast, as good as invisible. They hurtle up and through the stratosphere, and then fall where fate or luck or God or whatever you want to call it decrees.

It's four hours since we got the call that something had struck the Heurtebise Warehouse. A day-late Christmas lunch in full swing in the fire station, the radio at the maximum the volume knob will allow, blasting out Sandy MacPherson playing carols on his organ, and roast spuds and brussels sprouts and a black-market turkey being served under the makeshift decorations. Shouting *bang* because there's no snaps in the Christmas crackers! Just about got a mouthful of everything, and then the alarm went and we were on our way. Swearing mixed with the jokes from the crackers and everyone saying wasn't it *frigging cold* just to mask the fear. Brittle laughter. Keep it all warm, love; we'll be back in a jiffy. Keep it all good and warm till we're home.

But deep down everyone knows sometimes you don't come back.

Our engine picked down Maida Vale, feeling its way with the thin light from the slits we're allowed for headlights at last. (Thank God for that: I can still remember the awful thud when we hit that elderly pedestrian near Archway. He didn't stand a chance. More people were being killed in road accidents than from Hitler's bombs in those dark days.)

Jokes and laughter dying as we approached the bomb site, words giving way to a dry mouth, a busy heartbeat. As soon as I saw the blazing remains of the warehouse, I knew it couldn't have been a V-2 because there was still too much standing. Oil bomb probably, to make that much flame. Or a doodlebug. We dragged out a hose and got it working from an underground tank, stepping round a bare foot lying in the street, an arm—the kind of horror show that comes back at you in the middle of lunch the next day and makes you feel bad because you didn't feel bad at the time. (It's only the unusual or fantastic that sticks some days, like that hit on the taxidermy shop: stuffed crocodile lying in the gutter, zebra head perched on the canopy of a nearby hotel looking astonished to find itself there.)

This evening just seemed a job of dousing down the surrounding buildings and containing, but then through a shattered window in the factory I saw figures in the flames. Five or six of them standing, arms raised curiously as if beckoning me, but not moving at all. None of them trying to run or turn away and shield themselves from the approaching fire.

I batted Oakley on the shoulder and pointed. He gave me

that solid nod of his, shouted to shift my blooming arse, and the two of us fought our way into the ground floor, under that pile of flame and burning timber and unstable masonry, the kind of *theatricals* we're not meant to be doing and the CO hates.

Two of the trapped figures were already burning, the flames serpenting along their outstretched arms, sending up black smoke, poor souls swaying to and fro—very, very slowly. My stomach lurched and I waved, screamed, *For God's sake get out of there,* then fought on towards them through the heat and smoke around us when they still didn't react. (Oh, Ellis, if you could have seen me then, my brother, you might take back some of those things you said about bravery and cowardice and the relative distribution of those attributes in the Black family!)

And then I heard Oakley laughing and simultaneously coughing up his guts as the fumes got to him.

He tugged my arm. It's just a load of dummies, you dummy! Let's get out before the whole ruddy place comes down on us.

I looked around bewildered, too slow to understand (as ever!), still fixated on saving the doomed factory workers. I saw the other figures catch light and start to burn, still not making *any* effort to escape at all, and pushed on through the heat towards them—and at last realized what that daft bugger Oakley meant. Turns out Heurtebise was a factory and warehouse for shop outfitting:

mannequins and display stuff like that. Just dummies.

Bloody dummy yourself, I thought, and turned to go, but a beam came thumping down between Oakley and me in a curtain of sparks, fire blocking my way, the heat hitting that intensity you know means you've only got a minute or so left. I turned, ran blindly towards the back of the building, and kicked through a smoldering door, and found myself in an untouched storeroom. Boxes were standing open, half packed, spilling up their contents: an entire crate of crooked left arms; a line of rounded-off female torsos; long legs with pointed toes; ghostly, unseeing faces waiting for wigs or hats—bodies!—to become something. A surrealist's dream.

An utter stillness there, strangely beautiful and yet gruesome too, like that image in Goya's *Disasters of War*. (Maybe I could do something with that for *Warriors of the Machine*? Could be a big double-pager—words wrapping around the bodies, maybe a monoprint?) Despite the heat building at my back, the sound of the flames biting closer, the scene held me to the spot, images fixing themselves in my mind. Wonder-full.

On the far wall my escape route: a fire door, but next to it a row of small, dark wooden drawers caught my eye. They were neatly stenciled with words to excite any artist, begging to be opened: BURNT SIENNA; LAPIS; VIRIDIAN GREEN. Paints? I opened the one closest to the exit, labeled CERULEAN, and found myself staring at a rack of neatly arranged glass eyeballs of the most wonderful, celestial, gorgeous blue, all presumably waiting to be planted in some dummy's head, but now, disconcertingly, hypnotically, gazing back up at me. I can't quite put it into words—presumably why Ellis is the writer, not me—but those blue eyes seemed somehow to *see* me. To gaze right into me, deep into my soul. As if somebody had just asked a vital question and was waiting for an answer. What a blue! Like when you look towards the horizon on a late summer's day. When I get the *Warriors* book up and running at last, I'm going to use that exact blue in each and every blessed image.

God knows how long I stared at those eyes. Probably just seconds, but that was the moment something clicked inside. As if someone had shouted my name and catapulted me from sleep. As if I'd just been looking at things for days, weeks, months, but not actually SEEING anything. And suddenly my own eyes were wide open. The blue staring at me . . .

Bugger it, I utterly forgot where I was, that I was in danger . . .

I suppose technically it was looting, but they would only have melted anyway, and I couldn't leave without taking something of that piercing blue vision with me, so I took off my glove, dipped my hand into the box of eyes. They were cold, really cold. Untouched by the heat of the firestorm all around. I hadn't expected them to be so cold. Took a couple of decent handfuls and thrust them into my pocket. Around fifteen or so. A Christmas present to myself.

Then everything roared back into life, the fire coming through the door behind me like a dragon, the beams overhead cracking thunder, and the sound of falling masonry that you soon learn in this job is telling you to get yourself out PDQ. I felt the back of my helmet becoming hotter and hotter, felt the fire through my jacket, vision going like I was on the edge of passing out, and bludgeoned open the locked fire door with my ax at the fourth blow and tumbled out into the backyard, coughing up all the smoke I'd swallowed along with a bit of Christmas lunch, trying desperately to find my bearings. Then staggered back round to the engine to report that the building was clear of people.

And all the time the eyeballs were clicking away in my pocket.

Thank God, Oakley said. I thought we'd lost you this time, you daft sod. There's still Christmas pud to have! He tried to laugh, but his face was white. No jokes now, just relief and the exhaustion that comes towards the end of a shift.

And indeed here I am, still alive. I'd normally be shattered, but instead there's a kind of agitated excitement throbbing through me. Like I should be somewhere else or have forgotten something. That fiddler keeps playing steadily. Feel like I've heard that tune recently, but I can't place it.

I can see him now: a slim shadow leaning against a building on the other side of the street, loose strands of the white horsehair on his bow flickering in flame light as he picks out his melody. The water from our hoses is snaking down the street past him, slick with oil, pooling, flowing around the bodies and parts of bodies still lying in the street: a left hand disembodied, little finger cocked as if holding a cup of tea at the Café Royal. A head and shoulder and arm, the face turned away from me towards the fiddler. Nobody else seems to see him but me . . .

• • •

Something *has* changed. For the first time in ages and ages (first time since childhood?), I have realized that I am alive. Not just walking and breathing and talking and thinking, but really *alive*. I know it's not enough that I just survive, that I am still breathing. That's not living, is it? I need to make my life matter, my work matter, to see things clearly . . .

I want to write down what's happening, and in detail—not just scribble notes alongside my drawings like normal. My new project will be an artist's book, text and images together, as strong as I can make it. As I go through the dark streets of London, I want to describe each precious moment and try and make something that's powerful and true from all this. The flames and bright stars and glittering river that defy the chaos: I want to make them sing! Too many false steps in my life so far.

So *now* I shall begin to live. And maybe that will help me put matters right with my brother. Maybe it will give me the strength to say the things I want to say. Because I *need* to say them. Can't take the pain of this rift any longer.

And because I can't sing for toffee, I'll rely on what I can do: draw and write with new conviction so that I can create something that will live independently of me. Even if Father has washed his hands of me, even if Ellis thinks I'm a waste of time right now, I'll make *Warriors of the Machine* my weapon against all this nonsense around us. A New Year's resolution, a few days early—and one that I mean to stick to with every last little bit of my energy and strength. With the urgency of brushing fire from my head.

Oh! I've got these fifteen-odd eyeballs clacking away in my pocket, and they can be my witnesses. Yes, I like that!

Death comes two ways, as I say: either with the rumble and sudden warning engine cut of the doodlebug, or silently; with the V-2, you're blown to bits before you hear the roar of its engine and the sonic boom struggling to keep up. Three thousand miles an hour, Oakley said.

Three thousand bloody miles an hour.

You never know it's coming. So make the most of each and every moment.

Everything is strangely calm. No yesterday, no tomorrow. No Christmas Eve and no New Year's Day either. Just the sound of that violin and the stench from the factory. The water from our hoses coils towards the fiddler and makes a pool there before trickling away blackly down the street, trying to find the distant river. The grit and filth of Kilburn transformed. I feel a kind of *elation* running through me.

• • •

Time to head back.

I'll leave one of the glass eyeballs here, tucked into a crack in the brickwork.

And here I will begin to live.

———————————

Becoming

_____

I've died so many times it isn't funny anymore
(and after the first death there is no other),
but nevertheless,
it must be said
that I have learned a little more from each one.
One should walk through many lives, I think, before
    starting to judge, before making pronouncements,
    before saying this is this, and that is that, and the biggest
    judgment of all: *You should ... You! You should ...*
And I had to learn that lesson the hard way ...
A very hard way.

Here's a thing!
A thing to ponder,
something to make you sit and wonder:
a paradox, perhaps,
or just a trick,
but
until you have been someone else,
how can you know who you are, yourself?

Of course, that is only something I realized
   when I died for the first time.
Or, to be precise, when I began to live again,
   through someone else's eyes.
Because that was when the dance really began,
as I swung through the years with a querulous voice,
always trying to sing my song,
and now and again I was able
to step inside someone's mind
and whisper their name.
Harry! *Harry!*
Can you hear me?
Do you know who I am, who's calling you?
It's Orpheus, Harry, *Orpheus.*
I've come to call you to yourself,
to make you wake,
to help you see.
And the most important thing is that *you* are me.
Not yet, perhaps, but you will be when you wake,
when you open your eyes, shaking at the things around you,
trembling just from seeing the world at last.

Harry!

I saw you at the warehouse.

(Wasn't it *coward* that your father called you?)

You and Oakley, fighting the fire.

(Didn't your brother call you a *shirker?*)

I know you heard me, Harry!

Push through the door, Harry.

Leave those lifeless workers behind

and push through the door.

Become me, Harry. Become me,

and then the adventure can begin.

And then . . .

Something I hadn't foreseen.

You plunged your hand into a box of blue . . .

_____

6:45 p.m., Fire station 36

The station is quiet like it always is after a call. Everyone is knocked out with exhaustion or has slipped off somewhere for an hour or two's sleep. Oakley's wife was waiting for him and dragged him away home with a bright smile to hide her fear and relief. I'm being let off the last hour of my seventy-two-hour shift, for being *a bloody liability,* the CO says. My hand keeps reaching for the eyes in my pocket—desperate to pull one out so that I can gaze into that intense blue. There is something soothing in it after the heat and commotion of the factory fire. The unspoken question is still there when I do take a peek at one of them. And I still can't get that fiddler's tune out of my head. Sure I know it!

A note from Ellis was waiting for me along with the cold left-overs under the paper chains and streamers.

Meet you at the White Horse tonight, E.

And he's the one who wants to be the writer in our family!

Or used to at any rate. All going to waste now like everything else—and no spare words for me, it seems.

Feels like I did these Christmas decorations a lifetime ago. You're the art student, the CO said last week. Make it bloody well festive. So I had set about painting a night sky on the Prussian-blue blackout paper plastered to the hall's windows for the duration. Planets and constellations, a golden fiery comet and a special wandering star made from foil on the eastern horizon, to herald a new beginning. Seems we still have a little chunk of our normal lives amidst all this chaos, despite the gloomy predictions of the Yank officer I met in the White Horse on Christmas Eve.

Christmas Eve! Two days ago; seems like a million. Everyone doing their best to celebrate, to forget *there's a war on, don't you know?*

The Yank was glad enough for the pint I'd bought him, I remember, and no wonder given how hard it is to come by at the moment.

Heard the rumors? he grunted, squinting into the bottom of his beer mug.

Rumors?

About this new weapon the Germans are working on. It'll wipe this place off the map in a fraction of a second.

I told him I reckoned the V-2s were Hitler's last throw of the dice, and it would all be over when the launch sites in France and Holland were overrun (just parroting what Ellis told me to look like I knew what I was talking about), but the American just shook his head.

That's what they said about the V-1s, right? Something worse to come, kid. Always is. Always will be. Forever and ever, and amen.

Like what? I said.

He raised his eyebrows, gazed up at the dark ceiling above us—the kind of face that always knows better. Delights in the fact.

Some kinda supersonic beam, he grunted. Know a coupla guys at the Ministry. They reckon it's not far off. How old are you, kid?

I told him.

God, he said, and sighed. I remember being nineteen and a bit—and then raised his glass. I'd make the most of it if I were you. And a merry damn Xmas. X marks the spot!

I nodded and looked around again for Ellis. He was meant to turn up that night, but never did. I tried, really tried, to put away the disappointment and anxiety (and yes, relief) and not let it show on my face. When I looked back, the officer had slipped away into a knot of women haranguing old Greene the landlord, their voices ragged and calling him a Scrooge, threatening to rough him up good and proper if he wouldn't give them another drink.

Any more of that, ladies, and I'll bar the lot of you, he growled, winking at me. But the women just laughed harder and said they'd take some stopping once they got going. I don't doubt it.

I scribbled a note for Ellis—*Meet me here on Boxing Day?*— signed it, *Your little brother,* and slipped it into Greene's sturdy hand as I left.

• • •

Keep thinking about that fiddler and that tune—lodged in my head. I should have gone up to him and asked what he was playing, but when I'd reeled in the last of the hoses and turned to find him, he'd gone. Maybe Oakley knows it; forgot to ask.

I can get to the White Horse before Ellis arrives.

If he arrives.

Find us a nice quiet table in the corner and work out what I need to say—all part of the resolution to live fully, to leave nothing unsaid or undone, and try to heal the wound between us. It used to be you couldn't slide a cigarette paper between us, people said—the Black lads against the world. And now? Now it's a chasm that's widening with every passing day. One day it will grow too big. Or one day one of us will be gone and it will be too late. So . . .

Hopeful I can find the right words, but I feel nervous. Once you've said something, you can never swallow it back down. And I always say too much!

Or not enough.

Never the right amount.

Butterflies in my stomach along with a cold turkey sandwich and some manky sprouts.

Boxing Day, 7:45 p.m., White Horse

Still waiting for Ellis to show. A pint and a half in me and the pub jam-packed, noisy, but I want to keep a clear head. Good to have something to do; I'll write these notes and look busy, look like I've got things sorted.

It's all so complicated between E and me now, and yet it used to be so simple: the two of us playing in the stream beyond the hazel copse. Fighting pretend battles as knights or cowboys, when I thought nothing of raising my toy gun and blasting away at anyone and anything. Older brother included. The starlings rattled in and out of the clacking trees as we ran and whooped and screamed the sounds of death and dying. Making up our stories together as we went.

Had fun, boys? Father would say, and ruffle our hair if he was in a good mood. (If the order book was looking strong and the factory was gearing up for increased production. And if not, if the voices of reason and moderation seemed to be winning, then he would be silent and locked up in some internal—infernal?—calculation about material costs and labor rates and how many bombs the Ministry might want at a minimum . . .)

Would have been easier just to follow his plans for me. Into the family business and be part of the machinery of Black and Company, turning metal and chemicals I don't understand into intricate, perfect devices for the shortening of life. Just couldn't do it, though. I wasn't even sure why, at first, just knew I couldn't sodding do it. Some other blood must run in me! So now Ellis is angry and hurt and dismissive of his little brother who wants to play with paint at a time like this. Who went before a tribunal and got himself registered as a conscientious objector when the summons came. Who didn't quite make the grade to be an official war artist and got assigned to Fire Force 34. An embarrassment. (The black sheep of the Black family!)

And yet I know we can *both* still remember that togetherness. I do, and I believe he does too. I feel it, even in the worst moments, even if we can't say it, but . . .

I could do now with *hearing* the right words. I *need* to hear them. After that last bust-up at home, I fear I've burned too many bridges, been too stubborn, too sure of myself. It's beyond useless with Father. I can live with that, but maybe it's not too late for

E and me. Truth is I still need him. That brother of mine, who could write poetry as wonderful as those poems he wrote about Orpheus . . . That man can't have gone for good, can he?

Those women are back again. One of them screaming out a dirty joke about a V-2 and Goebbels and turning her glittering eyes on me. (Joke funny enough, but not that funny! And probably anatomically impossible.) Damn it. It's going to be: *Why aren't you in uniform, love? You're young. You look strong.* Do I tell them the truth? Or dodge it with the damaged lung thing?

Maybe Ellis is right: maybe I *am* a coward.

Put my head down and draw them, and hope he comes soon. Might tell him about that fiddler. He'll like that. Well, he would have, when he was still writing. He'd have spun at least one decent poem out of it, and that could have been the start of a string of poems. How could he give all that up? How on earth can he think, *It isn't the time to be messing around with art?* We need it now more than ever, like Chaplin said.

A bloke just told me drunkenly, *The fog's as thick as blooming sheep's wool out there.* That was good. Also that pubs are *stat-ist-i-cally* (he had some trouble there) the most dangerous places in London right now. Looking at those women arguing furiously, you could believe it, but he meant because of the bombs. Obviously. Apparently you stand more chance of being killed in a pub by a V-2 than any other building, though why the Nazis should be picking on public houses of north London he was at a loss to explain.

That tune still running around and around in my head.

Here's Ellis . . .

Orpheus in the Underworld

It may be instructive,

before we proceed,

to issue some lines of history.

It may be as well,

before we go on,

to talk of events that are now long gone.

This,

this, then . . .

. . . this . . .

. . . is my story.

The tale of what happened to me,

Orpheus,

your humble servant.

But even before we begin,

there are problems.

For I never had just one tale,

since no one ever told it the same.

Some said this, while others said that;

some told it well,

while with others it fell flat.

And we don't have long;

I must soon return to Harry and his song.

This is his story, *his*. Not mine.

Though as I said, they intertwine.

So I'll tell you the version that I like best.

Simple, it is; there's nothing to it.

Allow me now to walk you through it.

I've already told you about my song;

that's one thing everyone's agreed upon.

And most will tell you how, on my wedding day,

my wife, Eurydice, was taken away.

Bitten by a snake, struck down dead.

Persephone came for her, and led her

down to the Underworld,

to dwell in the dark

of Hades' kingdom.

Forever.

I was left.

Bereft, unable to be,

unable to sing for months on end,

determined to win Eurydice's life;

determined to be restored to my wife.

I journeyed into the Underworld,

and that part too, every one tells;

how I dared to venture into Hell.

There was more, much more, but . . .

That's enough.

That's enough for now, I think.

Because I left Harry on the brink

of meeting up with Ellis, his brother.

And do they still know how to love each other?

Have they forgotten their common blood?

Will they greet each other as they should?

That's something I would love to see.

So I return now,

eagerly.

———————————

10:45 p.m., on the bus.

Amazingly, the number 354 bus is still running. We're bumping over cracked roads, wheeling round heaps of darkened rubble, going at a clip. Not sure we're heading the right way, if I want to get back to my current digs, though! Mrs. Hudson will be hopping mad if I wake her and her husband up again coming in too late. At least they respect my stance. Not many do. And three weeks is the longest I've stayed anywhere this year.

We are *definitely* going the wrong way. Muttering from the back of the bus, and the driver just called out to say if anyone knew a better way to Hampstead, they were welcome to *come and have a blooming go* themselves, and he wasn't about to try the Great North Road because someone said there was a *dirty great hole* in it. Big explosion now towards the East End. You can feel it shake the seats. More still to come tonight? Already launched? Already in the dark skies above?

Rockets or not, bumps or not, I have to jot this down before I forget it all. The conversation with Ellis was more intense, more troubling, than I thought. But good to have had it, good to have tried rather than dodged—and maybe it even helped a bit.

So.

He looked better than when I last saw him in the hospital. Felt a surge of relief to see those hollowed-out cheeks of a month ago had filled, that his color was back. As for the wound, he said the plate's doing its job on the bone, the scar is dry now, and he'll be right as rain. And then he can head back across the Channel and do his bit for the push to Berlin. That was his opening salvo—the last words emphasized to give me a slap—and then silence for a bit until I proposed we drink to each other's health, and he nodded. So we did.

He looked at me. That steady gaze that says, *I know just a little better than you.* An extra year and six months of wisdom!

What did you want to talk about, then? he said. I don't want to rehash all the old arguments about Father and the rest of it.

Why not? I asked.

Because it doesn't get us anywhere. Never will; waste of time.

Silence. Then:

You've let people down, Harry. A bloody *conchie* in the family! Aunt Vanessa even thrust a white feather at me to give you when I saw you. As good as blamed me!

She's an idiot, I said, she always was—and tried a joke instead. You should tell her I *nearly* rescued some shop dummies today in Kilburn.

He made a face and looked like he'd rather be anywhere but there, and I veered away. Easier topics first, I thought, maybe some idle gossip to build some bridges. What did he think about the rumors of a new German super weapon, for example?

Rubbish, he scoffed. Absolute tosh.

That's what some said about the V-2s, I argued. People wouldn't believe them even when the first ones hit.

He nodded, a slight concession.

I reminded him how last year everyone was talking about the four-hundred-ton glider bomb. Terrified it was imminent. That's exhaustion for you, or the fact that the end's in sight and suddenly you can't believe you'll make it. So people have to invent some new horror. Like that mysterious hum people are going on about. I hadn't heard about it until the other day, but apparently there's been a stack of reports of a steady, pulsing drone that sounds like it's coming from under the pavement. People hearing it all over

London. Audible at night when there's a gap in the attacks: a throbbing deep underground. Supposedly.

What did my big brother make of that?

Ellis shrugged. Collective tinnitus. Hysteria. Morale's worse now than in '41; people will believe *anything*.

So it's not a supersonic ray, then?

Engine testing. Nothing more, trust me.

I'll sleep easier in my bed, then, I said, changing tack—and told him about the fire at Heurtebise's, the burning mannequins, the eyeballs, the fiddler. I saw his attention sharpen at that, creative senses sniffing out something valuable like they always used to. Once a poet always a poet, the "bees of the invisible" just like Rilke said and which Ellis quoted at the start of the collection he was working on. Can't deny what you are, brother! I thought.

But then his face changed. Your mannequins make me think of that ghastly waxwork display in town about Nazi atrocities, he said. Pandering to base instincts. Grubby voyeurism.

You're right about that, I agreed. And then told him I was trying to do something better, that I've started working again, making drawings and notes for a book, an illustrated book, a book about war and machines. I think it could be important, I said, getting carried away as usual. Maybe you could do the words, and we could see if anyone was interested in publishing it and—

No time for that stuff now, he snapped, giving me the big brother look.

But people will listen to you, I argued. You've had poems published in magazines; you won that competition, for God's sake.

He shook his head. There's no damn paper for one thing! And I've got nothing to say right now.

Then he softened again, just a bit.

Who knows, though? He sighed. One day, maybe. When all this is done and we're older . . . I thought you'd given up on being a war artist.

Too young apparently, I said. Too inexperienced, and they've got enough big names on their lists, Moore and people like that. I'd still do it, and happily, best way I could help, but those men at the War Office didn't want a student.

Help? Ellis said then. How does it help to *draw* things? I mean, in these days?

I looked at him and paraphrased that line from *The Great Dictator,* said that right now we think too much and feel too little. Art helps us feel and make sense of things . . .

My voice trailed off. We neither of us said anything for a while, sipped our drinks while the pub grew louder around us. A pretty young girl in a Wren uniform was giving him the eye from the next table. He looked at her, then back at me.

Tell me about it anyhow, he said, quietly.

So I told him, told him that I want to make something that counts, something from deep inside, and went on about the fake eyes and the fiddler again. And I must have got the enthusiasm to him, because for a moment it was like it always was and he listened, properly listened, ears pinned back, as I told him about the dummies burning, the building sending up fire angels into the darkening sky. I built it up and then told him about the eyeballs in detail, and suddenly, like a magician, I pulled one out, at just the right moment, and set it on the table, where it spun like a small blue moon, taking in the saloon bar, the ragged women, the soldiers on leave. He stared at it, biting his lip thoughtfully. I knew I'd got to him, the lovely bastard. At least in that moment.

Ellis smiled and rolled it back across the table to me.

Do you remember a song that goes like this? I said, encouraged. And did my best to sing that slow lilting tune the fiddler played.

He scrunched up his face. No. I don't think so. Maybe. Are you getting it right?

I'm not sure. It just seems so familiar, but I don't know what it is.

He listened a few bars more and then shook his head. Drained his pint and lit a cigarette.

What did you really want to talk about, Harry?

About us, I said, grasping the nettle. I want things better between us. In case . . .

Father says you've let the *whole* family down, he said impatiently. And I have to say I agree with him. You've been high-handed, high-minded. This is the real bloody world, Harry, and we've got to fight for it. A real enemy, this is about as black-and-white as it gets.

Tapping the table with his index finger for emphasis, that hard look back in his eyes.

I am, I said. In my own way.

Running around playing fireman with a lot of other shirkers!

I mean painting, I said. And those *shirkers* are saving lives, by the way, and it seemed like the best choice on the list for objectors—

His words flung back: For God's sake, Harry! Do you know what's going on across the Channel? Do you know how many people are dying because we didn't do enough to fight when this could have been nipped in the bud? If you saw that waxwork's display, then you know about the camps. The gas chambers.

I don't want to argue about that, I said. I want to talk about us—

Father is cutting you out of his will. You know that, don't you? You're waving goodbye to an inheritance, Harry. A lifetime of security.

Father can go hang, I snapped.

He grimaced, then said, Fine talk for a pacifist.

Well, the last thing I want is *his* money, I said; it's got blood all over it and he can shove it. You're both welcome to it!

Way too hard—Ellis was already on his feet.

It's not that you're a coward I mind, he said. It's that you're so bloody smug about it.

I don't mean to be, I said. Maybe I was just born that way.

You could still do the right thing. Father's not the monster you paint him to be.

But I'm making a new start, Ellis, I said. And I wanted you to know that. And that you matter to me. More than ever really, but I don't want you lecturing me. I'm doing what my conscience tells me to do. Can't you respect that, if nothing else?

His shoulders sagged at that, and he stood there for a long while, then nodded slowly and sat back down again. Raised his glass silently. Someone started to plunk away at the piano, a ragged version of "Lili Marlene." Or at least that's how it started, and then it seemed to slip into something else, a meandering tune that reminded me of that damn fiddler again.

I wanted to hear something back, or add that I loved him—part of the whole resolution of vowing to live FULLY and honestly—but couldn't say it, of course. And I'd risked enough and sparked a little connection there. Rescued the conversation from it being just another step towards us drifting so far apart that we can never be together again.

And maybe he felt that too, and things eased as we charted the way back to easier ground. Even chatted a bit about Christmases long ago in the Shropshire snow, sledging down Foxes Hill as the light faded and the trees turned black around us. We both loved that I know, our half-German mother singing her beloved carols "O Tannenbaum" and "Süsser die Glocken," and the sparklers fizzing in the tall fir tree. Her face reflecting them as the match caught, glowing, so full of life. Shadows of the last war, her fears of another and what was happening across the North Sea in her homeland brushed away by that dancing light.

I think I wrote my first god-awful poem about that, Ellis said with a half-smile. It had some bloody terrible rhymes! Probably even *holly* and *jolly*! And then his face turned to something more somber. Poor old Mutti. She wouldn't have wanted to see all this, though, would she: what's happened to Germany. The thousand bomber raids on the Ruhr and Cologne. Maybe it's almost better this way.

I nodded, raised my glass to her memory. She'd have wanted us not to be at war with each other, I said. You and me, I mean.

Mmm, he said. She'd have not wanted you to have said those things to Father either. She'd have been appalled.

I thought about arguing again but didn't want to do that over Mutti's memory, so I raised my glass again and drained it and wished him good night.

He nodded. I liked those eyes, he said. I'll give you that!

And then I left him and the pretty Wren, who had nestled at his elbow now and was giving him the once-over. Bringing out all the charm and ease and wiping away the war and the rest of it for at least an hour or two.

Outside, I took one of the eyeballs and, climbing up on the window ledge, tucked it in a nook on top of the White Horse sign, where it sat, surveying the darkened street, the board swaying in a sudden cold breeze. As if the air was only moving down at the pub, not along the street, a great *swoosh* of wind making the fog dance and whirl about. In a blackened-out shell of a building across the road, shredded net curtains billowed from the empty windows like pale wings. And then everything went still again. Very still. The pollarded plane tree on the corner seemed a silent watcher, its knobbly, stunted fingers reaching out over me.

I tried to listen for that mysterious hum, but could hear nothing but voices and laughter spilling from the pub, the distant *poom-poom-poom* of an antiaircraft battery beating time with my heart. Piano plugging away inside. Dog bark. The steady growl of a doodlebug came dragging across the sky overhead, and I waited and waited, listened for the cut out of its engine, getting ready to dive for cover, but it just went on trundling its way northwest. My number not up yet!

Does this idiot driver know what he's doing? We're going round in circles. Surely we're at the top of Kilburn High Road again. Maybe I should just go back and have another drink with E. No, don't want to interrupt him.

A few dark shadows pass on the street. Timeless. Towering ruins of bricks that were once river clay deep underground and are heading there again. In blacked-out wintertime London, it's as if you're underground more than half the time. Are the silent passersby alive? Do they know they are alive? Maybe they just think they are. Maybe we all just think we are! Maybe I shou—

———————

Harry?

Can you hear me?

Haagse Bos

Holland.

Houtland.

Die Hout.

The woods.

Here lies the Haagse Bos;

all that remains of the ancient wood from

    which the country gets its name.

A vast rectangular park — surrounded by city;

still it provides miles of forest in which to hide.

That is: in which to hide *things*.

The tall old trees have lived longer than anyone alive; they've

    seen some sights, and dark deeds have happened down the

    years under the branches of the Haagse Bos: robbings,

    hangings, knives in the back. But nothing as dark as this.

Look! Under the trees; there are long cylindrical shapes lying.

Rockets. One hundred and two rockets.

Rocket bombs for London, just two hundred miles west. Two

    hundred miles, or to the bombs: five minutes' flying.

The woods are forbidden lands now,

only the men in their asbestos suits

pass beyond the soldiers at the edge of the trees
to bend to their work around this theme of death.

Curious, a horse with no more owner wanders by.
A pale, muddy horse.
It stops and watches the men,
looks up at the sky,
lowers its head, walks on again.

Here, on the crossroads of well-worn riding trails, sits
    a Meillerwagen, a mighty six-wheeled beast, from
    which the weapon can be raised to point at the sky.
    Forty-six feet of technology, towering to the treetops,
    hidden from view of all but the few antlike creatures
    who make final arrangements from the radio car.
From the city comes a cable, two miles long, along which runs that
    watery fire known as electricity. Snaking into the park, under the
    trees, across the dead leaves from the previous autumn, supplying
    power to the wagons, so the bomb can be brought to life.
Then, after hours of preparation, a finger, that has been
    hovering above a button, does not hesitate.

Ignition:

Liquid oxygen.

Hydrogen peroxide.

Sodium permanganate.

Eight tons of alcohol and water.

Electricity.

The rocket pushes out of the forest,

blasting the ground for ten yards round.

Rising slowly from the trees,

scorching the leaves,

it leaves behind a billowing cloud

of dark gray smoke

and is gone.

At a hundred feet up

a jet of flame erupts from the rear,

and it turns towards its target,

trailing vapor in its wake,

a spiral trail of vapor.

A smear.

The fuel disappears.

It develops   speed.

Just sixty seconds later, the engine cuts out

and the rocket is fifty miles high skimming the black edge of space, from where it begins its descent in parabolic free fall.

Gaining more speed, and more, till at three thousand miles an
     hour it arrives at the White Horse, where those wailing women
     have just departed, leaving Ellis and the Wren and forty-two
     other souls who know nothing of its coming. It moves faster
     than its own sound, so that it is in a moment of silence, as if all
     noise has been pushed away, that the rocket reaches London.

Detonation:
Ammonium nitrate.
Tri-nitro-toluene.
Electricity.

Instantaneously, the White Horse no longer exists.
The sound of the explosion, joined now by the rocket's roar that has
     caught up at last, is like the heart being torn out of the earth.
Those bricks that are not instantly pulverized into clay dust
     are hurled outward from the blast along with other items:
shards of glass,
timbers of wood,
fragments of metal,
and things that were people.
The air folds in on itself,

vibrating as if the gut string of a giant lyre

has been plucked.

The White Horse no longer exists,

and those who were in the saloon bar have gone.

I'm sorry.

I am Orpheus, the singer. I wanted to sing this to you, but I cannot

    sing of such things. The music dies on my lips, never gets

    started. I just want to close my eyes, hold the palm of my hand

    towards you, and let the music flow, like a loving energy.

But it won't.

Do you know where those bombs began?

Not in a forest in Holland.

They began underground,

in a tunnel in a Teutonic mountain, two miles deep.

There — in tunnels storing poison gas and kerosene — was where

    the bombs were built. Slaves, living in the dark, in dusty tunnels.

    Forced to build the weapons that would be used against their allies.

Now, the bombs have returned to the Underworld,

    and there is no song for that.

I watch. I watch the roiling dust and the tumbling obliteration, and

    my fiddle feels cold in my hands. I want to sing, but I cannot.

I, who can charm the rocks, cause water to change its course

    with my song, I, who once charmed Death himself,

am powerless. I should have sung the rocket from the

sky and sent it soft to the sea, but I could not.

There is no song that can tame these monsters.

The Machines.

I am Orpheus, and I am old, yet even I am not old enough

to know how we began. Did we climb down from the

trees, or did we slime our way out of the seas? Or did we

emerge from a cave or from under the ground?

Who were we? What were we like? And when did we begin to speak?

What a moment! That was when I was ready to be

born, when words were ready to be sung!

But how quickly did singing come? Was it soon, or did it take

an age? Did we have music before we had words? Did we have

music before we had *tools*? And what were those tools?

A stick, perhaps, or half of a shell. A broken flint.

Or maybe the jawbone of an ass.

Yes? And what was it used for? I don't know, I don't know, but I can

guess. (And I further deduce that it was the male who showed

the way on that front. Of the female, I will say more later.)

From there, where are we now? Nineteen hundred and forty-

four, as Harry would know it. No jawbones anymore. No

need for such primitive tools. We had spears and swords

when I was a boy in Thrace; now they have guns.

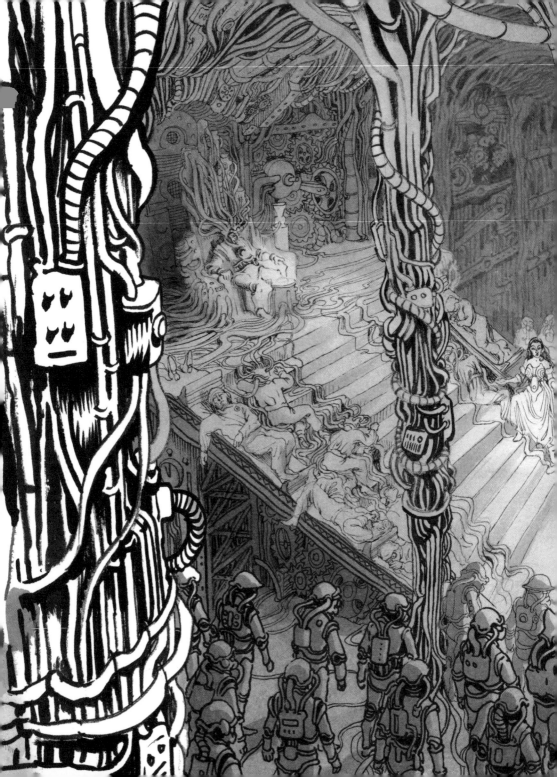

And gas.

And doodlebugs, rocket bombs.

Planes that make the cities burn,

ack-ack guns to bring them down.

Radar that sees what no man could;

machines that go where no man should:

submarine warships that slide in the deep;

deadly torpedoes that glide in the dark.

And pistols and rifles and mortars and mines,

and tanks to pulverize enemy lines.

Oh, see that I am starting to sing.

But is it right to sing of such things?

Is it wrong?

And from here, where will we end?

What *machinery* will we create?

Already the Earth hums from far underground,

some thrumming sound

that will have penetrated into the deep

and woken things it were better let sleep.

All of London trembles on this terrible vibration.

Some hear it. Others choose not to:

those for whom fear is too much to bear,

and it's easy to pretend you just didn't hear.

Into my mind spring visions of barbarous mechanisms.

I don't yet understand what each of them is; I see bombs much
    smaller than these V-2 rockets, yet each with the power to
    obliterate a city, and I ask myself, How can that be?

I see missiles that can cruise halfway round
    the world, but how can that be?

I see planes that can fly faster than sound, demolish
    a village and return to an airfield that floats on
    the sea. How can all these things be?

My imagination does not stop:

Here's a plane, just a few feet wide, far too small for a man inside.
    Its pilot is sitting in a comfortable chair, thousands of miles
    from enemy shores. She navigates by signals beamed from
    tiny moons encircling our Earth. She flies using science and
    then, with the stroke of a key, a town far away ceases to be.

She tidies her desk and gets in her car, drives home to her
    children, her husband. They laugh and they chat, then
    fall into bed where she sleeps without dreaming.

How can *that* be?

More visions are coming, but I push them away. Enough
    for now, enough. My song is broken and weak.

Harry! Harry! You must wake up soon.

Still I'm waiting for you to be me,

for you to open your eyes and see,

for you to open your mind.

And Harry, if you don't open your mind

    soon, I will open it for you.

I, or maybe . . . maybe the war will,

because more than one bomb falls on London tonight.

Kilburn.

It means Cold Water; cold water that springs from the

    earth. And beside this river an ancient trackway from

    ancient days, as men came with their cattle to London.

Kilburn:

Time passes; a metamorphosis occurs.

The river returned underground and only the name

    remains to remind us of what was once here.

Kilburn:

Regular rows of handsome streets.

Shops and houses and pubs.

And here comes a bus, number 354.

And Harry's on board, right at the back, when out of the

    sky with a sickening smack, a rocket bomb drops,

drops with brutal power.

It lands at the spot where Cavendish Road meets Kilburn High

    — and the houses for a quarter mile around no longer exist.

The bus rears into the air like a frightened horse, then collapses
   onto the tarmac on its side, as the powdered remains of
   Cavendish Road flow over it like a dirty river to nothing.
   The driver of the bus has disappeared. No one comes to help;
   this is a night of common destruction. No one stirs.
The bus had been almost empty, save for the driver and . . .
There.
At the back, twisted under a seat.
A man.
Blood flowing
over sharp metal
sticking from the skull
with no shame at all at what it's done.

Harry?
Harry?
Can you hear me at last,
now there's a hole in
   your head?

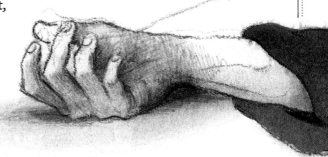

27th of Dec.? 28th?
9:15 a.m.
Hospital bed

Nothing made sense in the dark, nothing but a ringing void filling my head. I struggled up from the depths, seeing nothing, understanding nothing.

Sheep's wool!

And then I was awake, something like awake at any rate, and I lay still for ages, regathering myself. Waiting. And now I'm trying to understand a new reality.

So. I started with the *immediate* again. With senses. Smell came back first. Disinfectant stinging my nostrils, soap, a vague tinge of something burnt. Next, sounds: footsteps hurrying past, then gone, a drawn-out groan from much farther away. An owl! Then sensation returned: the ache, the ache in my head, throbbing away, drowning everything out for a long, long while. When at last I managed to open my eyes, it was to see a nurse hovering at the foot of my metal hospital bed, angel-like. She was no more than a silhouette on the darkened ward, her face a pale oval.

You're still with us, then, she whispered. Glad to see it!

The first thing I said: Where's my notebook?

Don't worry about that now. Just rest.

I need it, I said. It's important. What happened? Am I dead?

A gentle shake of her head. Not yet! It was a V–2. You were lucky! Or unlucky . . . Your bus wasn't where it was supposed to be. Rocket was a direct hit on a pub and the blast rolled your bus clean over.

Which pub?

No idea, she said. You'll have to excuse me. Coming in thick and fast at the moment.

And she hurried away. That was hours ago. I slept more, and now it's morning and I feel like I can write a bit. Still that urge to record things even though my head feels so queer. I see my notebook beside my bed.

The last thing I remember before the rocket strike is the fiddler at the Heurtebise factory. After that my notes have to fill in the gaps. No recall of the conversation with Ellis, which I read now as you would a novel, wondering what comes next. Good and bad, I see. No recall of boarding the bus. Or how we ended up back near the White Horse and—

I'm getting muddled. She said a *pub*. She didn't say the White Horse. There are more than one or two pubs in London, after all. And I was miles from there. I think. *I think,* but I can't be sure. That's scary, the gaps in my mind, in my memory. If you lose your memories, then what have you got left? What are you?

Head hurts. Feels like something's not working right in there. Too tired to write much more.

Was the pub the White Horse? And was Ellis still there? Oh God. I felt as if I were in some race against time to put things right—now maybe I'm already too late. I'll ask that nurse to try and find out for me.

Someone is whistling. Same tune that the fiddler was playing? A janitor down the corridor. Why can't I place it? Blurred sparrows (seven) puffed up against the cold on the windowsill in a line, opening their beaks as if joining in. And something else: a rumbling sound? A deep resonant hum, just at the threshold of hearing.

12:45 p.m.

I slipped back into sleep, or was unconscious again. I don't know if I can tell the difference right now. But it felt very deep, time-less — and then I came rocketing up from the depths. In a panic. My first thought was for Ellis, of course, but almost immediately after that I thought of the eyeballs and had a sudden urge to check if I still had them. Groped blindly in the pocket of my jacket hanging beside the bed and felt huge relief to find them still clacking away there. Cool. Reassuring.

Want to write more now, find out more, but not much strength. They wheeled a chap away from the next bed, covered over completely, gurney squeaking down the corridor to wherever it is you go when they cover your face. So much for living fully — maybe it's just a matter of staying alive!

The whistling janitor watched him pass, bowed his head, then said to me, Cheer up, mate. Might never happen.

Me: I think it already has. Where are they taking that chap?

Janitor, with finality: The basement.

I nodded, asked him what tune he'd been whistling.

Janitor: I heard some bloke playing it the other day. No idea. Lovely though, ain't it?

Me: Can you hear a kind of humming sound?

Janitor: Yeah. The generators are on the blink.

But that wasn't what I could hear, I'm sure. Maybe the explosion from the rocket's done something to my ears. Need to find someone who can go and check about the pub. About Ellis.

December 27th, 5:20p.m.
Royal Free Hospital,
C Ward

Feeling a bit more alert now — and at least I know where I am. And what day it is. Another deep sleep, and then a harried-looking doctor did a thorough examination and shone lights in my eyes until I saw bright suns, and made me do some sums that were easy enough, and they redid the dressing on my head. The doctor gave me a reassuring smile — might just have been habit.

Strange though: when he asked me my full name, I stumbled for a moment. It was on the very tip of my tongue, but then something else nearly came out. I had to fish around for the word "Harry" like you would for something dropped down the back of a closet. Daft. They gave me some more morphine and a couple of pills. Pain seems to have eased but it feels really odd, as if there's a space in there. A big space.

A fragment of the bus ride came back, though: I was on the 354, the driver a silent silhouette wrestling with his huge wheel, and I said, Where the hell are we going? And he said, Just back to the blooming beginning again, mate.

The blooming beginning. Can't think straight.

5:30p.m.

It *was* the White Horse.

Annihilated, the nurse just told me. Annihilated. Sounded wrong coming from her mouth, I thought, and, at the same moment, Oh God, my brother's dead.

But I don't actually *know* that. They're still digging, apparently; and anyway, he might have left by the time the rocket hit. I asked the nurse if she could find out more, and she patted my hand and said she would do her best.

God, I wish I knew.

Feel I was ages and ages on the bus; Ellis and that Wren would have hopped it by then, surely? War hurries us all up. Worried sick about him, but nobody's got time to check it out for me. Wounded coming in like the clappers from all over town.

Going to do a memory drawing of the bus driver in the hope it jogs more. And to try and put my fears to one side. That night ride through the darkened ruins felt like a part of the story I'll tell in *Warriors*. Something very old, something mythic almost. The driver must have been blundering around, trying to find a road that wasn't blocked or punched through, but how strange that we ended up back where we started, just in time to meet that V-2. Well, like my teacher said, if you want to make sense of the world, damn well draw it. Things always feel better when I can get hold of them with pencil and ink. So:

Dec. 28th, 10:20 a.m., Royal Free

Desperate for news from the bomb site. Need to know about E. The rocket would have obliterated the pub and everyone in it. That's your V-2 for you: sudden, total, absolute.

The friendly nurse came back, said she could spare me a few minutes. I'd like to draw her, stop me thinking about Ellis. But don't think I could do her justice. Plain face, but in a good way, and a dimple that would normally lift my spirits. Told me what she had found out, and my worst fears were realized. I knew when she smiled that it wasn't good; it was the smile Father gave us when he told us about Mutti. Then a cough, a long pause, and the words: Ah. Look, boys, about your mother . . . I need you to be strong. Something died in him after that—and we were left to deal with it all ourselves.

If Ellis was still in the pub, then he's dead, the nurse whispered. Totally destroyed in a direct hit; they pulled out only one survivor, an old man, and the rest were killed on the spot, they reckon. Forty-three bodies so far and they're still digging, but no hope of finding anyone else they say.

She put her cool hand on mine again. Maybe he left before it hit, she said. A lot of confusion after these things.

I'm beside myself, I said. I need to get out of here and take a look.

She shook her head. Not a chance. Doctors are rather worried about you, you see. Your head took an awful bang.

She looked at my drawing of the bus driver.

You an artist, then?

Trying to be. What's your name?

Eunice.

Well, Eunice, thing is I'm more worried about Ellis than I am about myself right now.

I know, she said, and smoothed the back of my hand, wiping tension away there — as if she knew a secret that lay just beyond me (a secret, I feel, everyone else knows) — and then walked off down the sun-blinded corridor.

Now through the windows I can see the bright cold morning. Smoke lifting in twenty different tones of charcoal and gray into clear blue air. The barrage balloons are shining silver, like they're pinned to the sky. Astonishingly beautiful really. And those sparrows whirring away on the ledge. And the worry and that blessed hum rumbling away nonstop in my ears.

Don't feel physically too bad. Just worried sick.

Think I'll go and take a look at the bomb site. Ask around and see if anyone saw Ellis leave. Don't even know where he's been staying these last few weeks since they let him out of the hospital, but someone might be able to tell me something. Can't stick around here, waiting.

I vowed to live, and you can't live fully lying around waiting for some doctor to tell you that you can go and look for your brother.

11:45 a.m.

Some escape bid! Didn't get far before I was apprehended; and now I'm back in bed feeling foolish—and as woozy as anything. Clock on the wall is a bit of a blur when I try to look that far.

I'd only reached the back stairs when the world started turning around me faster and faster. Reached for the handrail for something steady and heard my name being called. The same flustered doctor took my arm and chivvied me back to bed with all kinds of dire warnings about hemorrhages and such and then sent Eunice to read me—with that dimpled smile—a version of the riot act.

To be honest, I didn't feel that well as soon as I stood up on my legs. Felt like it does when you use your left hand for something you normally do with your right. Like I'm not myself somehow.

But I had an interesting encounter on the way, before they caught me—and it felt moving, important.

Need to put it down as I have a growing fear that the void in my head will enlarge and start to snuff out thoughts and memories, or muddle them up, so I need to get the important things down in this book. If I start forgetting, then this book can be my memory, a portable memory. It's a comforting idea.

The encounter: I lost my way trying to find the stairs and ended up in a gloomy back corridor, the wards half empty and quiet. Went through a door clearly labeled EXIT and along another even quieter corridor, as if that part of the hospital has been closed off. Thought I could hear that humming more distinctly there, easier to pick out in this silence, like it was coming up through the bones of the building, as if I were hearing it with my feet like ants do. Some of the windows were broken, and cold clear air streamed

in—and then I heard a young girl's voice singing. I recognized that melody at once, and the words. A German nursery rhyme: "Hoppe, hoppe Reiter." Mutti used to sing it to us when we were little (which, can you believe it now, Father loved hearing), and I felt happy and sad all at once, astonished to hear it in this place, and followed it round the corner to a four-bed ward to find the girl half propped up on her pillows, singing away and staring at a photo in her hand. Tangled dark hair, pale skin, her face the shape of an apple pip. A long, slim hand reached out from under the covers gripping the photograph. No one else there. As I drew closer, I saw her fingers were trembling slightly.

She broke off the rhyme and looked up at me.

Hello, I said. Are you all right? Aren't you cold in here?

She shook her head. I told them I wanted some peace and some quiet, she replied in slow, careful English. I am warm enough. Thank you for asking me.

German? I asked. *Ich kann Deutsch sprechen.* Sort of.

I do not want to speak German now, thank you, she said, emphatically, and lay back on the pillows, the hand and the photo she was holding dropping to the covers.

Are you in here for long? I asked. Can I fetch you anything?

Not so long, she said. I want to get out and go and look for my parents. I'm worried.

Where are they?

Not far away. But I am worried about them.

Do they live close by?

She shrugged and then said this: How to explain? You go right and left and then straight on. And then there is no direction anymore.

I struggled to understand. Do you mean Hackney?

Ich weiss nicht. Then she scowled at herself for using German.

You're sure I can't fetch anyone? Anything?

She shook her head and then turned to me again and gave me a look of such earnest intensity that it shook me to the core.

Like she was reaching out and grabbing my hand tightly.

Will you leave soon? she asked.

I hope so, I said, dragging a smile to my lips. I'm looking for someone myself.

Who?

My brother.

What has happened to him? Is he in trouble?

I don't know. I think so.

She sat up a bit again, that beseeching look back on her face. When you go, you *must* take me with you. Do you promise? I want to go.

I told her I wasn't sure it was a good idea.

But you must, she said urgently. It is important! *Sehr wichtig.*

Again she scowled. I didn't know what to say. Then footsteps echoed in the corridor outside, and I knew I needed to get a move on. My head was swirling, the dizziness already gathering.

You must take me with you, she repeated. I am ready. I am fine.

What's your name? I asked.

Agatha, she said. What's yours?

And it was the queerest thing. I couldn't bring my own name out straightaway. Again that gap in my head as I fumbled around for it. Again that feeling of wrong-handedness, and I found a short stream of syllables tumbling from my mouth.

Orpheus, I said.

And then corrected myself, stumbling, blushing even. No, I'm Harry. Harry Black, National Fire Service—and she laughed at the flicker of bafflement that must have crossed my face.

Her look said: *Are you quite sure?*

Quite sure, I said, tapping my head lightly. I've had a bash, I explained. Things getting muddled up.

She nodded thoughtfully.

I pulled myself together, wanting to help her, to lift her spirits. Asked her if she'd like me to keep an eye on her. And gave her one of my looted blue eyeballs, and she took it quietly and closed her long fingers around it without another word. She understood that it didn't need to make sense. The way children do. The way adults sometimes don't, if they've forgotten the direct business of early childhood. Storytelling.

An eye, she said, with a half smile. Keep an eye. I like it. *Danke.*

I asked her how old she was. Fourteen, she said. How about you, Harry?

Not much older, I said.

I keep seeing her face as I lie here now. I'd like to draw her. Apparently they need to knock me out again and take a look at the wound. But as soon as that's done, I'm off. Why the hell did

I say *Orpheus*? Must be some memory of Ellis's poetry surfacing. I never told him just how great those poems of his really are. I wish I had.

Daft, like I said before. Morphine maybe, scrambling me up like an egg.

If only we had real eggs instead of the powdered stuff.

December 29th, Early morning
(I think)

Inky depths. No dreams. Nothing. Maybe some of that sheep's wool fog. I get the feeling for a while I wasn't anywhere at all. Just drifting.

Remember the orderlies coming to fetch me, and we were on the way to the operating room.

In the corridor we passed that girl—Agatha—and I said, Ah, you're up and about, then; and she said, I told you: I'm fine now. I'm ready to go; I'm just waiting for someone. That photo was still in her hand, I noticed.

Wish me luck, I said.

You do not need luck, she replied, fired me a quick smile, and then turned to the window, the barrage balloons, the bright winter day.

I told her I'd come to visit as soon as I'd had my head looked at.

Keep still now, there's a good chap, one of the orderlies said. You're not making much sense.

They wheeled me on down the corridor, and then there was dazzling light and the roar of the respirator like a hurricane wind in my ears and quiet voices murmuring—and then a quick *fade to Black*.

———————

Psychopomp

———————————

Harry!

You heard me!

For a while there, you knew who you were.

You used your true name.

I'm so happy I could dance!

Ha!

Now we are connected, I can show you some things.

I can show you the operation they're performing on your head.

Would you like to see that?

There's a lot of people, the pump of the respirator,

and even more blood, and—

You don't want to know?

You don't want to see?

I'd be desperate if it were happening to me;

and remember, Harry, in a way, it is.

For we are one now.

All right, then.

I'll show you something else,

what you're longing to see above all.

The way I live now is a marvelous thing.

A thing of freedom and boundless expression.

I get lonely, of course,

in the solitary times

when I am between minds,

but now I'm alive once more, in you, and we can go

    places and see things and be there in the smallest

    smattering of time; all we have to do is dream.

I know where you want to go, Harry.

I know who you want to see, Harry.

I am the psychopomp; the guider of souls;

and I know where you want to be.

Look. Here it is; this is where the White Horse stood.

Don't recognize it?

You've seen enough of these things to know how

    the world can change in an instant.

The pub was here, and the grocer's there,

and Abraham's bookshop was somewhere around.

Look, there are even books that survived the blast,

while others are now just pages that flutter and curl,

their stories leaving,

leaking into the dust that was London.

But we haven't come to see books.

Look, Harry, look!

There's a crack in the Earth,

through which you can see the Underworld.

And can you see who's down there, Harry?

Can you see him?

He's alive, Harry. O gods, he's alive!

That's what you wanted to see;

that's what you wanted to know.

He's alive, Harry.

Your brother is still alive.

Listen to me now, Harry.

Don't say it can't be true.

Everyone else was blown to bits.

He can't be down there.

Harry, don't be so logical!

Stop trying to analyze things

that are beyond understanding.

Don't try to rationalize that which cannot be understood.

If you do, you will lose me again.

Remember me, Harry,

Remember . . .

And know one thing:
It wasn't the morphine that made you speak;
It was me.

That's good.
You've understood.
You've stopped trying to know, and started to be,
just like you and Ellis used to be free,
as children of the Shropshire hills.
Now we can work wonders, you and I.
As one.

———————————

December 29th, Evening

Back in bed. Takes me a while to realize I'm not at my digs with the Hudsons but in the bleachy wards of the Royal Free. Head feels better now under the bandages, though everything seems muffled. Eunice and another nurse just went past, and I heard her say that it was snowing a bit. Sudden image in my head, a burst of memory: standing in the bay window at home in Shropshire, I must have been no more than six or seven, and squeezing in between the long curtains and the cold, condensated glass and staring out into the night as the snow fell. Blanketing, muffling the hills of the Marches. I stood there mesmerized, almost terrified by the depth of the night, the weight of the snow, but also elated. Somehow, trapped halfway between inside and out, I felt invisible to everyone, as if I were disappearing into the snow, the darkness. And Ellis came looking for me, and when he found me, instead of teasing me and dismissing my reverie, he fell into silent companionship beside me, our breaths fogging rough heart shapes on the cold glass.

Can't bear to think of him out there, maybe trapped, maybe worse, under the rubble and freezing fog. Must get out of here and get to the bomb site and try and find him. PDQ.

I wonder if I can just pull this drip out? Wait till morning or go now?

Agatha's face in the corridor. Should I stick up for her? If I don't, will she be stuck here until someone comes to claim her? Her parents must be looking for her—if they made it, that is. Poor thing, I suppose they'll just put her in some home or something. I keep seeing that look she gave me and the way she seemed to be wanting *my* help. Mine, and nobody else's.

Remember the resolution. Live and live fully. I'll give myself a couple of hours' more rest and then I'm going, and bugger the consequences. I have to know what's happened to Ellis.

One good thing: Oakley came to visit, and I was really glad to see him. A bit of solid (very solid!) reality amongst all this chaos in my head.

You OK, then, mate? he asked, dragging up a chair.

I told him I wasn't sure, that I thought I'd nearly not made it . . .

Remember Archway? he said. That blast that knocked me off my feet?

I nodded.

Oakley was a coalman before the war, strong as the proverbial bloody ox, absolutely no nonsense about anything. But that night in Archway, we had found him out cold, thought he was having a heart attack, lips blue and face all white from the gypsum. Took a long and ghastly age of pumping his chest before we pulled him back.

He leaned close now to my bed and whispered, Well, Harry, that night *something 'appened*. Really weird. But I didn't want to tell anyone. Not at first.

He cleared his throat.

I've been wanting to tell someone for bloody ages. Thought you'd understand. You're different than the rest.

Go on, I said.

And hesitantly he told me how, after the rocket blast and the blacking out, quite distinctly he felt a part of himself separate from his body and float up very, very gently above the scene, over the rest of us huddling around, and rolling him into recovery, over all the *fuss and bother*.

I was twenty or thirty feet up — like I was on a bloody extension ladder, he said, but I didn't feel anything, just really, really calm as I watched you lot panicking around me like headless chickens. I felt like I was off to somewhere else, above the barrage balloons that were shining overhead, and I thought I could just cut one loose and float up with it all the way to heaven — or past that to somewhere else even better. Somewhere over the bloody rainbow!

He stopped and looked at me, alarmed, as if he felt he'd said too much. Then he forced a smile. Don't tell a soul—or I'll do you in.

Cross my heart, I said. Glad you came back to us, though.

So am I. He smiled, swatting my knee hard. And don't you damn well think of going nowhere without me, you bugger!

Later

Dead middle of the night. I'm awake and can't sleep. I was deeply asleep, and then I felt someone tapping away at my hand, where the drip goes in. Tap, tap, tapping away. Thought it was Eunice or the doctor and growled at them to leave me be, but the finger kept jabbing away, and I opened my eyes to find Agatha sitting on my bed, looking at me, her voice rising in volume like someone was cranking up the knob on a wireless.

Wake up. Wake up, Harry. Wake up, Mister Orpheus. Wake up . . .

The conversation was so . . . odd . . . that I want to put it down as verbatim as I can before I forget it.

I asked her what the matter was.

You cannot keep lying here, she said. You have to go and look. You need to find your brother.

I nodded and asked her if she was supposed to be out of bed.

It doesn't matter, she whispered. I will go back in a minute before they notice me gone. My parents might possibly come tonight, and if they do, I do not want to miss them. I need to be with them.

I had to ask: So your parents *are* with you? Here in London?

She looked at me with that intense gaze again.

It is complicated, Harry. They wanted to come because it was not safe back home anymore. My father said we had to go. They send me on a train first, and they were going to follow me soon.

Smart chap. But do you know if they are in England?

She nodded. Yes, they are close. If they do not find me, then I will find them. You will help me, perhaps.

So they didn't bring you to the hospital?

No. Some men with an ambulance.

What happened?

A big explosion. I was trapped and covered with white stuff. They got me out, breathe into my mouth.

She pointed at her lips then, the strangest little gesture, as if I wouldn't understand without.

Where were you all?

She shook her head then and gave me a brave smile. I cannot remember.

Only to be expected. Must be the shock of being caught in a blast or concussion. If the ambulance boys gave her the kiss of life, then she must have been in a bad way. Guess they're keeping her in for observation for a while; she looks right as rain, apart from the pallor.

She smiled again: Mister Orpheus, you will help me find them?

Stop calling me that, I said. But if you were on a Kinder-transport, you must have been here a while already?

Quite a long time, she said. I am waiting for them for a long time.

I told her I didn't understand, but then she heard footsteps coming, and she turned and tiptoed away on the darkened ward.

At the last moment, she glanced over her shoulder and—in a fierce stage whisper—fired me another volley: You should get out of here and start looking for your brother. But don't forget about me, Harry.

———————————

Closing Time

The hospital is quiet tonight.

A good night for mischief!

A good night for a jailbreak.

The dimpled Eunice comes by and chats to Harry for a

    little while, and I watch, trying to stifle my laughter as

    Harry pretends to be sleepy so she'll leave him alone.

As soon as she's gone,

he pulls back the sheets,

and pulls on the clothes they've left on a chair.

Slides on his shoes and slips from the bed

to the waiting window, where —

Where he stops, leg halfway over the windowsill.

Agatha.

He made a promise to that little girl,

and suddenly it seems important that promises are kept.

He comes back into his empty ward,

takes the door to where he saw her before.

But she's gone.

Her things are still there, so she's not been discharged,

not been discarded, nor died in the night.

But he has to go;

he has to find Ellis.

He makes a silent promise to the hospital air

to return for her,

then slips into the night.

———————————

Dec. 30, Dawn, Site of the White Horse

Here in Maenad Road, someone's made a fire from the wrecked timbers, and I'm sitting by that, blanket pulled around my shoulders, shivering like a newborn animal, trying to make sense of what's happened, numbed and shocked, trying to find my bearings. A dirty tumbler of whisky beside me that I'll have another go at in a minute. But now I need to get this all down. Something reassuring about the whisper of a sharpened pencil across the paper of this journal. It's anchoring me, warming me as much as the blanket and the drink.

The world has been turned completely upside down here. Not a stick or stone of the pub left that I can see, just a huge blast crater tumbled with rubble and debris, smoke rising from the heart of it, the snow settling on the edge but melting in the smoldering wreckage. Teams of women and older men are relaying the remains of the pub and the houses that stood on the corner, working quietly in the dawn light, bundled up against the cold. A dog sniffs at the edge of the crater — looks a bit like our old Lottie. Very similar, in fact, tail busy as she scratches away at something.

I realize I have lost my watch somewhere. Must have been in the blast itself, or maybe someone took it off me in the hospital; but it wasn't with this notebook or my wallet on the stand by the bed. Well, what is time anyway? Artificial. Relative. A tyranny for men and women. Do the trees care what time it is? The sparrows? I reckon not. I'll live without it for a bit.

Overhead the sky looks like porridge. No sign of the house that stood opposite with the net curtains flaring. Not a trace of the big old plane tree that erupted out of the paving stones on the corner. Where the hell has that gone?! Launched into space? (Remember Dalston: that lead coffin that got hurled about two hundred yards from the cemetery. God, that stank when it burst open; only time I vomited on duty.)

Some books on the ground.

Not a trace of Ellis.

Have to fear the worst now after what old Greene just told me. (Yes, Greene dodged this particular rocket, it seems.)

My escape from the Royal Free went better this time. My head felt good, Agatha's encouraging words pushing me into action.

I bided my time until Eunice made her last round, feigned sleep and waited until her footsteps were gone and lost against the hum of whatever it is that is humming—and then pulled out the drip, dressed, grabbed this journal, and made for the window. Then I remembered my promise to Agatha.

I dodged back round past her room, maybe to take her with me, maybe just to wish her well—but she wasn't there. An orderly was coming down the corridor, so I tried to look as though I wasn't a fugitive and asked him where the German girl was.

Don't know about no German girl, he said. Are you supposed to be in here?

No, I said—and walked briskly away before he tried to stop me.

Odd. Got out by the back stairs as the shimmy down from the window looked just too much.

I reached the bomb site as first light came up. Found Greene standing at the rim of the crater that's in front of me now: hands planted on his hips, gazing into the middle of it, mouth open as if he were on the verge of saying something, but no sound coming out. His face was covered with white—gypsum probably—like you always see at rocket sites, the impact so great it pulverizes plaster and throws it over everything and everyone, but it always gives you a shock when you see it. Makes people look like the dead uprisen. I tapped him on the shoulder, and his eyes were big and dark in that white face.

It took him a moment to recognize me — and then he shut his eyes and groaned.

I'm sorry, lad, he said. Really sorry.

I asked him what happened, delaying the question I was desperate to ask, already knowing what the answer would be.

Popped home to see the missus, he said. I just had a feeling, a *funny* feeling, so I went home to tell her to take the nippers and go to the shelter. I was heading back when the thing hit. I knew right away it was the Horse. Shook like billy-o, the whole ruddy street.

Me: Do you know if Ellis was still in there? My brother?

He didn't hesitate.

I'm sorry. I'm almost sure of it. Unless he left in the five minutes I was gone; he was deep in it with that pretty little

Wren . . . I've not seen them pull his body out, mind.

He sat down then on the rubble, abruptly, at a complete loss, shaking his head, struggling. That big bear of a man gasping, holding back tears.

But your family's OK? I asked, numb.

The missus and the kids are fine, he said. But . . . He gestured at the crater, but they were all family too, all that lot in there. We're all bloody family round here, even the ones I can't stand.

His eyes were shimmering, hands clenching and unclenching. I patted him on the back, suddenly felt very cold, chilled right to the heart of me, and found this blanket on an unused stretcher, and whipped and wrapped it tight around. Then picked my way down into the ruins of the pub, the air stinging with smoke, eyes watering, and a damn awful smell that I didn't want to name.

Found myself calling Ellis's name, shouting, Where are you? But my voice wouldn't work properly, and it came out as a kind of strangulated moan. Like someone trying to sing who hasn't sung for years. A creaky old man's half-remembered song. There was a rolling roar of a blast from the East End then, and the rubble sifters stopped and looked up, but I just kept going, wallowing around in the tumble of bricks and smoldering timber, banging my shins, shivering like buggery.

The moon hung pale over us in the half-light.

Me, a lunatic.

Just then, the damn postman came down the street. He barely paused, just took one look at the rubble, then spotted a box at the end of what's left of the street, a red finger sticking out of the dust. Calm as you please, he went to open it and take out the letters. Posted by the dead, probably, and now their last words have outlived them. But their last letter has survived. *Yes, thank you, we're all well. Tom's turning two tomorrow. Of course, these nights do give you the heebie-jeebies, but Nan says God will protect us and who's to say she isn't right?*

Yes, as I say, after what Greene told me, I have to fear the worst. And yet, standing there . . .

What was it? Something tickled in my brain. I don't know how else to describe it. An impulse stirring, like when your body knows it has to do something that your head has completely forgotten.

I fumbled in my pocket and took a blue eyeball and dropped it in the chaos at my feet. It skittered off a broken piece of brickwork, rolled down a bit of corrugated iron, and plopped through a hole into darkness, some hidden emptiness beneath. It fell and I didn't hear it hit bottom.

An image flashed in my head, though, a firing of the imagination seen as clear as the hand in front of my face, as if very, very briefly I could glimpse my brother, lying there below us. Somehow close to me, but far, far away at the same time, the image there for one blink and then gone again in the next.

And I shouted at the top of my lungs, like I was trying to burst them out of my chest: Ellis! ELLIS!

Some Civil Defense chap with a mustache that must have irritated even him took me firmly by the shoulders and guided me back up to where Maenad Road should be, and told me that the bomb site wasn't safe and the cellars under the pub could give way at any minute. Might be other stuff under that, he said. Who knows what?

Bugger that, I shouted. My brother's down there. All the more reason to get on with it.

The mustache man twisted his mouth. If he is, then he's dead. Direct hit. Any idea what the blast from one of those rockets is like? No unclaimed male fatalities on my list from the bodies they recovered. We need a heavy-duty crane now.

He looked back at the center of the blast, counting off the body count on his sausage fingers. A lot of women, two Wrens, a Yank, two Polish boys. Lots of other bits and pieces we can't put together.

He peered at my head, at the bandages. What happened to you?

I was on the bus, I said. The 354.

Bus? he said, frowning. The 354 doesn't run past here. You look white as a sheet, young man.

The shivers had really got me now, so I came over to the fire and sat down, and here I am.

Sparks shooting up into the early morning sky, a truck backing up to take bigger chunks of masonry off the road. A friendly woman from the damaged row of houses behind gave me this glass of some filthy whisky or other, and that's helping calm the shakes a bit. Still this terrible numbness like that wool stuffing up my head.

And now what? Think I'll join the helpers digging out the wreckage when these big bits of beam and masonry are shifted. If Ellis is down there—whatever state he's in—I want to be there when they find him. Just feeling a bit wobbly. I'll sit a few more minutes.

That dog really does remind me of our Lottie. Poor old thing.

And I keep thinking about that girl Agatha too. I think maybe I should help her—she looks like everyone has forgotten her.

Seems madness to draw now, but nothing else to be done while we wait for this crane. So . . .

———————

Kinder

I lurk behind Harry, looking over his shoulder,
watching the miracle marks his pencil makes,
and I peek at the paper and then at his subject,
and then I stand back, and say, Well!
What a thing!
If I had a hat, I'd tip it.
No!
I'd take it off and throw it into the sky.
Harry!
You're a wizard, a magician of sorts;
and this is the true intensity of your magic,
for you don't draw things as they really are:
you draw them as they *deserve to be seen*.

Well!
What a thing!
He's drawing Greene!
The man whose pub has just been destroyed.
Look! There's his head,
and there are his arms.

And look at the way he's doing the boots!

Ha!

Well!

What a thing!

And . . .

And, and . . . ?

Well,

not too far from where Greene stands

lies a single shoe, lost by a child.

Harry's seen it — he starts to draw.

And this is the power,

the mystical power of Harry's skill,

for in that shoe I see a million things.

I see girls like Agatha;

boys with no name.

I see children dispatched

on overflowing trains;

I see the trains plowing through darkening rains.

I see families split, broken apart.

I see their worn-out hearts.

I see the tears, I see the dread,

I see the fear inside everyone's head.

I see men like Greene with guns in their hands;

I see men like Greene taking careful aim.

I see men like Greene dropping bombs from planes.

And I see men like Greene

trying, yes, they're trying,

to make the world whole

again.

That's the power of Harry's art,

and if you only see a fraction of it,

well, that's a start.

———————————

Later

Was surprisingly OK while I was drawing. As if a guardian angel had a hand on my shoulder, steadying me. Often the way; but now that I've stopped, the shakes are back along with that gnawing fear and grief in the pit of my belly. The sun is rising up over the battered horizon, shifting rays coming through the smoke from the crater and the fire. I can feel its warmth creeping through all that cold space between it and me, helping my fingers to work. Funny thing: as I scribbled away at the shapes in the wreckage, an image started to form in my mind.

I always try and make the things that you could fudge — clouds, trees, waves — as accurate as possible, and then you don't run the risk of missing something vital in front of your nose. Some tiny detail that will explain why the world makes you feel shaken and moved. There was a shoe, a child's tan shoe, its lace missing and tongue pulled back against the uppers, and I drew it, and the crane and all that. But the rest, the heaps of charred and

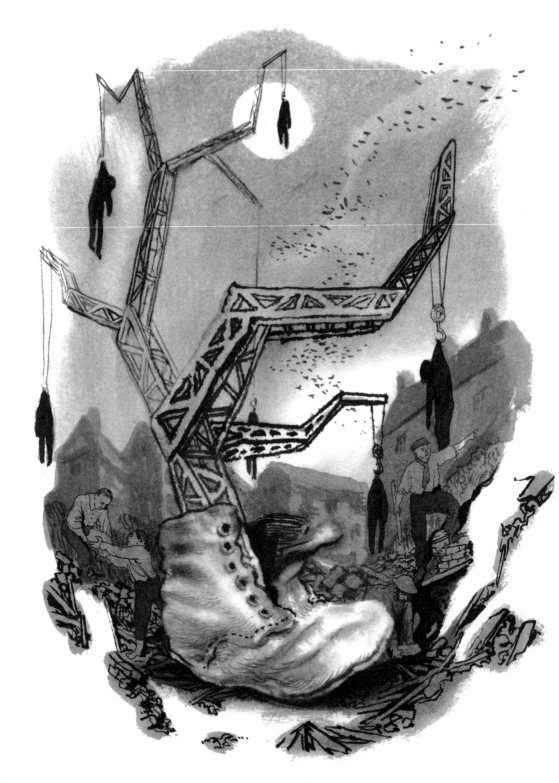

pulverized building, seemed just too confusing to draw, too dizzying to understand how something as solid as the White Horse could be reduced to all these constituent, random parts in a handful of seconds.

Yet the more I concentrated on drawing the broken bricks and smoke and rescuers and Greene poised at the very edge, immobile, the more I *felt* Ellis. His presence, argumentative, paying compliments (backhanded, like always), chivvying me along. *Come on, H, do something useful. Call that a bloody line? I thought you were supposed to be able to draw! What are you waiting for? I'm here, brother. Right here when you've done messing about.*

Morphine again, I suppose, and my imagination working hard in the void. Conjuring him. Can't believe he's dead. Therefore he isn't. He was meant to be the indestructible one always, the tough one. The fighter.

P.S. Just heard it again: a violin singing, beyond the blast radius on the far side of all the rubble and ruin. I worked my way around to see who was playing and blow me down, if it wasn't the same fiddler as at the warehouse fire. I'm sure of it. Different tune, though, lively, upbeat, making my toes move and tap along, almost wanting to dance despite everything. The very same man for sure, wreathed in smoke that was curling up from the bomb damage and swirling round him with the stiffening breeze. There was a gaggle of street kids staring at him, and now they started to move, clapping their hands, woefully out of time but getting enthusiastic, warming themselves up.

I shouted, Has one of you lost a shoe? Tan one without a lace? It's over there. But they all just looked at me as if I was a bit touched and kept dancing.

Good that he's lifting their spirits. Maybe some of them lost a relative or a neighbor in the blast, yet here they are dancing. I wanted to wait for the fiddler to finish and go and ask what that tune was he was playing the other night. Feels like it matters. The kind of thing that once I'd have rushed to share with Ellis before all the awkwardness got in the way. Coincidences, things that stand up suddenly in front of you and salute the mind. But the fiddler didn't seem like he wanted to stop and the children were having a good time, so I just scribbled it down best I could. I'll finish this (feel compelled to finish this), then get digging with the others.

Funny thing is, my hand keeps trying to draw lines that aren't there. Feels like if I let it off the leash, it would go crazy, like a dog with a fresh scent. Like our Lottie chasing rabbits on a hillside. Feels as if I would need a massive sheet of paper, double elephant or bigger, and would fill it. Maybe I'm not right in the head after all. Strong ache there now from the wound again, and Eunice's warnings coming back at me. And doing that last drawing, I had a horrible moment of double vision and everything blurred.

Seven urchins, linking hands now as they caper around and around the fiddler like mad things. A bit dizzying, but then I suddenly think how much Agatha would enjoy something like this. She seems so quiet and contained, and she needs to feel some warmth and movement. Some life!

Come on, H! It's like I can hear Ellis in my head again. *Better get cracking.*

Well, time to dig. I feel pretty rough, have to say, but I can't wait anymore.

So . . .

———————————

Spellbinder

And dig, Harry did.

I watched him from across the radius of death,

while I scratched a tune on this old violin,

a fiddle I found in the first of the blasts,

when I was new to the city and wide-eyed with wonder.

It's a terrible instrument but that doesn't matter,

for I could make music from any old thing,

from the beat of a heart to the twang of a string

releasing an arrow;

and besides,

the children I played for

were sweet little sparrows,

who could have danced in the dust till the war was done.

And then!

I saw Harry drop something into the deep.

A blue glass eye!

That was it: the thing I had not predicted;

that Harry would find a new way of seeing.

And then he dug, and shifted and lifted

and pulled. And then I saw him looking across at me,

at me and my spellbound kids.

He paused, and seemed about to speak.

Then his head swung up and his eyes rolled back,

and he fell to the ground.

Not dead!

Just spellbound too.

Some others came and carried him off;

an ambulance van came and took him away,

back to that hospital, both royal and free,

where he slept deeper than sleep and half as alive.

For hours he drifted, hours and hours, and I?

I wondered whether I might lose him, then.

I stood by his bed. One hand on his head,

feeling for thoughts, memories, emotions, anything.

And all I felt was the beat of his blood, and then,

just faintly,

a snatch of a song,

a scratchy old tune on a bad violin.

Then he coughed and sucked up a lungful of air

and I laughed and I swore like Harry himself.

Bloody hell, lad, but you gave me a scare.

I watched from the window when the doctors came by.
They scolded and chided and finally had Harry understand
that the wound in his head was deep, and bad,
that any motion could make it much worse,
that if he wanted to live he needed to rest.
That   they   knew   best.

And Eunice came when the doctors went, and
    reproached him as she had before, only not quite.
    This time, there was a softness in her voice, and
    a softness in her eye, which made me pause.
In that softness I felt a thousand things, of times
    long ago, of lovers lost, of a tenderness that
    cannot be described with words, only music.
And that is why I sing.

As I watched Eunice, I doubted myself.
Perhaps, Harry, perhaps.
Perhaps you're not the one for me.
Should I go and blow in someone else's ear?
Leave you to Love and let Ellis die?
Who am I to bring you to life?

You could get well and take this nurse as your wife,
live happily and long and remember your brother
as one whom you loved but who drifted away,
place a rose on his grave every hundredth day.

And then, Harry, you woke.
You decided, *you* spoke.
It was your doing, your choice,
and then I knew how strong you are.
You made Eunice blush with a kiss on her cheek,
and sat up in bed, and asked for a paper.
Something to pass the time, you said;
and indeed the time passed as you got out of bed,
and went and found Agatha
and fled.

———————————

*December 30, Evening,
deep shelter, Camden
Town Underground*

At last a moment to rest. A moment of stillness and a chance to put down the events of today.

We're sitting now, Agatha and I, in the warm hugger-mugger of a deep shelter, with the thump and roar of the rockets and buzz bombs just noises off. How many people down here? A couple of hundred, all inhaling each other's breath and odor. There's some quiet chatter, some snoring, laughter at the other end of the tunnel. It feels good to be down here, safe.

Makes me think of a wonderful poem that Ellis wrote in his Orpheus sequence, about a fox going to ground. About her *catching something cold on the wind*—the scent of a hound or a bugle—and racing away up a *hill of twilight, zipping the night up behind,* diving through the tree roots for the den and safety. *Into the arms of the warm earth.*

I always loved that *hill of twilight*—should have told him as much—and now I know what his fox felt.

Rocket impacts are making the ground tremble. It's a big wave of an attack, and they would have moved us out of the Royal Free tonight anyway, if we—Agatha and I—hadn't evacuated ourselves. So to speak.

After blacking out at the bomb site, I woke up in my hospital bed again, still digging frantically with both hands, trying to burrow down into the rubble and keep up that hunt for Ellis, yet finding myself scrabbling away not at debris but at the tangled bedsheets. Eunice hurried over, clearly alarmed by my state, and put me in my place gently. She said I was lucky to be alive, that I had *to listen to orders,* and then came back every hour to check. A lovely girl; she clearly likes me—and for a moment, just a moment, I thought about giving up and letting her look after me, and then maybe, when I'm better, we might go for a walk together . . . a drink . . .

But I knew that was for another time. Now I had to get going again. Ever since I saw those kids dancing in the smoke, I'd been thinking about poor little Agatha — and I could feel that need to resume the hunt for Ellis tugging at me.

So when Eunice came back for the third time, I sent her on an errand that I knew would take a good ten minutes, and then, like that fox, slipped away up my own hill of twilight. Or down the darkened corridor at any rate.

I found Agatha back in her room, sitting on the edge of her bed with her shoes on, and an overcoat buttoned up to her chin. She smiled when she saw me, a fraction of a second of smile, but a smile nonetheless. As if she had been waiting for me and had known I'd be there any minute.

There you are at last, she said. My Mister Orpheus.

I told her to *stick to Harry, for God's sake,* and she nodded as if humoring a daft teacher.

You weren't here when I looked in last time, I said. I was worried I'd lost you.

I can't go on my own, she said. I need someone to help me find my parents. And I think you are the one, Mister Harry.

Just Harry, I said. But do you know if they even made it to London? You didn't seem sure when I asked you the other day.

Yes, she said. I think so, by now. You will help me find them.

I know it. And I will help you find your brother.

She held out a hand, steady this time. We shake on it? An agreement?

It's a deal, I said, and took her hand in mine.

Me: You're freezing.

Recently I have bad — ach — *Blutkreislauf.*

Circulation?

She nodded.

There's something about this girl: for all of fourteen, she's very grown up indeed. I suppose that's what being put on a Kinder-transport must do to you. And there's something about her determination and her occasional lightning-flash smile that gives me fresh strength too.

So what we do now? she asked. Have you made up your mind? Are we going to find your brother?

Yes, I said. We're going to do what we English call *a runner.* Have you got everything?

She nodded. I have my photograph of my parents and that is all I need. I am ready for our runner. I always liked to run when I was little.

And that's what we did. My third escape bid, just like you read in the papers about POWs trying again and again to get out of

Stalag—whatever. Because they are determined to do their duty. Well, they're not the only ones.

As we made our dash down the back stairs, the sirens blared across town and a rocket attack came in. That helped us; everyone was going berserk and no one even saw us, let alone tried to stop us. We started towards the bomb site, but then a couple of hits very close by forced us to take shelter, jostling with the rest to flee underground, every bone in my body urging that direction suddenly, demanding we get below the earth, burrow beneath the city.

Ellis is still alive, I know it, and an inner voice keeps telling me I need to go down not just for safety, but to find him. And bring him back. As soon as the all-clear sounds, we'll head to the blasted bit of ground where the White Horse stood and start digging down into the rubble again.

Agatha was very silent as we joined the crowds making their way down into this shelter. Suppose she's done a lot of this since she came from Germany, and God knows what she went through over there. Even crowds might bother her, I suppose.

I told her she was brave as anything, and she just shook her head and gave me a smile.

When this attack is over, I said, I'm going to look for Ellis again. I should find some official help for you. You must be registered at a town hall as a refugee, and they might know something about your parents. Any idea where you have been staying?

I cannot remember, Mister Harry, she said. But you will help me find them?

Of course, I told her. I just don't know where to start. And first I've got to see about Ellis.

I will help you, she said. I want to stay with you.

Overhead there was a hell of a thud, followed by a throaty roar as something struck not more than a few hundred yards away. She squeezed closer to me on our bench.

Show me that picture of yours, I said to take her mind off the rockets, and she plucked the creased photo out of her coat pocket and gave it to me.

This is them, then? I asked, trying to lift her spirits.

She nodded.

Jewish?

She paused before saying yes.

A young couple in a sunlit garden, the sun bright on their faces and both squinting a bit. The man soberly dressed in a dark suit and holding a pale bundle in his arms, and the dark-haired woman looking at the baby there and smiling, reaching out with a finger to adjust the flowery shawl. Her dress is light, summer light, swept by a gust of wind against her legs. A fleeting summer breeze, caught by the shutter click and therefore forever.

That is me, Agatha said solemnly, touching the bundle in her father's arms with a finger that shook very slightly.

That really got to me, that little shake of her finger. Again that sense of huge agitation inside, like she's trying to contain it, like maybe she's been containing that for weeks or months or even years, and it might burst out of her all at once. The same urgency I'm feeling.

I'll help you find them, I said, and bloody hell I had to control the shake in my voice as I said it. I promise. But Ellis. He may not have much time. Understand? He might be trapped but still alive.

My parents will wait for me, Agatha said, looking up as another long rolling rumble hollowed down our shelter tunnel. Tell me about your brother.

He's a bit older than me, I said. Thinks he's a bit cleverer too.

But you love him, yes?

I nodded. I think he's going to be a great writer one day. If . . .

I jammed on my brakes and told Agatha to go to sleep, but instead she glanced at this notebook in my hands.

May I have a look, please?

It's just some rough notes, I said, and explained I was trying to make sense of an idea, doing preliminary drawings, but that the book had turned into more of a journal these last few days. She nodded, as if only half listening, and set about reading a page or two.

So, she said, you are a writer too.

Good God no, I said. Ellis is the writer. Won a real prize in a poetry competition and everything. And I doubt anything will ever come of all this. It's just me messing around, really.

She shook her head and went on reading for a while longer, and then handed the book back.

I like it, she said. My papa reads me a lot of English books. He used to teach at the university. I'm sure he would like this.

I told her I doubted it and asked her again if she had any idea where she was registered.

No, she said. I'm sorry. Will you write more now? I think you should.

Only to be expected that she can't remember these funny English place-names I suppose. She looks calm enough now, my little friend Agatha, but the toes of one foot are tapping away frantically underneath that calm. The last few weeks have unnerved everyone, and regulars in the shelter are saying they haven't seen so many people down here for months. Something so very chilling about this new threat we face. Rockets even now arcing through the heavens towards us. Once a rocket is launched, there's no way to bring it back again, and these new ones must only take a handful of minutes to cross the gray water of the North Sea and hit us.

Doodlebugs, buzz bombs, robot bombs, vengeance rockets—call them what you will, names do and don't matter—but what they are is dehumanized. And that's what's blooming well given me the willies, one woman said as we came down.

Dehumanized. Have to do something with that in the *Warriors* book. Make the machines weird and awful and deadly, and piloted not by men but by machines, which are ruthlessly efficient and have not even the chance of exercising a conscience. No awareness of what they are doing. Maybe they decide their own targets; maybe they're huge and powerful; maybe they're the size of wasps, swarms of them, or even smaller—must force this to the ultimate (il-)logical conclusion.

Now Agatha's fallen asleep, slumped against me, breathing evenly, rhythmically, and all that tension has dropped away from her tapping foot, though from time to time, she shudders and half whimpers something in German that I can't quite make out. Her right shoe is missing a lace; I'll improvise one for her in a moment.

The bangs and shudders have eased overhead, and I'm desperate to get going, but I have to let Agatha rest a while. She's beat.

Keep thinking about how that eyeball dropped through the rubble and ruin into the dark space lurking beneath. As if it saw for me! Father always said my imagination runs away with me, but I can't help feeling that's what happened. That sky-blue eye saw Ellis; he's still alive.

I'll give Agatha another few minutes and then we'll get going.

———

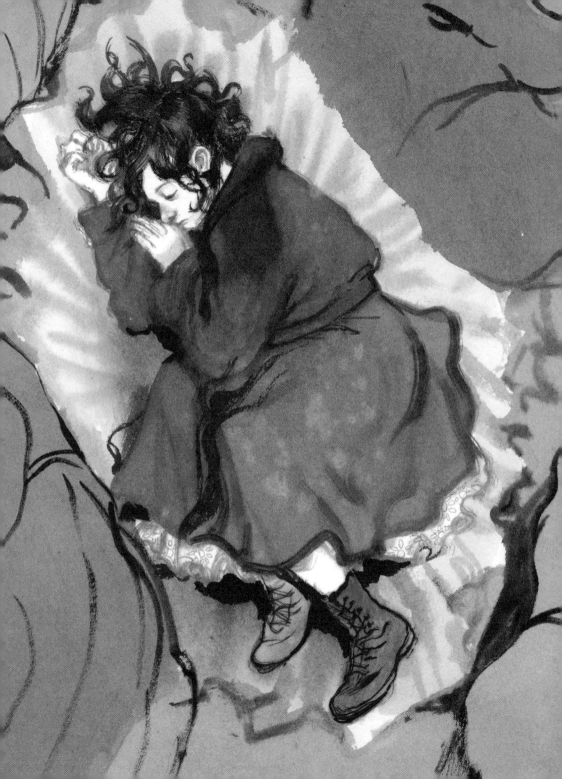

Sleep

Wolf-slaying wonder,
queller of thunder,
cousin of both life and death.

Nothing can touch you
as your mind brings you to
safety, as you slow your breath.

Sleep.
The original wonder,
a mystery deeper than anyone knows.
A heavenly gift
casts you adrift,
soothing the mind
outside of time.
In darkness you roam,
far from home,
while your body stays here,
right here,
resting.
Resting.

I could see the pain in Harry's head,
feel the ache in his arms and legs,
and while he allowed for Agatha's rest,
told himself that he knew best,
he wouldn't admit his precarious health,
wouldn't take care of himself.

And though he will know nothing when he wakes,
it was I who whispered in his ear,
and sang him a lullaby soft and sweet,
and took him down to blissful sleep.

Sleep.
So his body will recover.

Sleep.
So that he may grow.

Sleep.
So his mind can forget.

Sleep.
So belief can grow.

Sleep.

    Sleep.

        Sleep.

Wolf-slaying wonder,
queller of thunder.
Cousin of both life,
and death.

———————————

Later, Camden Town
Deep Shelter

Bugger it, fell asleep on my drawing and then must have slept for an age. Lights are all off and there's just a dim glow at the end of the tunnel. People cocooned around us, dead to the world, to whatever's happening overhead.

I dreamed I heard that fiddle music again, the slow tune haunting my sleep. It was coming closer and closer, and then a voice joined in singing—I couldn't make out the words, but it was getting louder.

And then I woke up. As if the voice and the song had woken me, but everything is so very quiet now down here, the darkness absorbing sound, stuffing itself into my ears. I can hear my heart beat. Nothing else. The attack must be over.

Huddled masses on the platform; shapes of things that are people. Above their heads on the tunnel wall government information: a cartoon pig asking for food waste, a scrap metal drive, *Loose Lips*

Sink Ships, and a few posters still up for vacations that will never happen: Bognor Regis, Weston-super-Mare. *Skegness Is So Bracing.* Showing a world that no longer exists (does it?)—the world of the living.

There's a door near us at this far end of the tunnel, a sign I can just make out in the gloom: STRICTLY NO ADMITTANCE AT ANY TIME. Stupid! *Someone* must go through it at some time!

There's a flashlight on the ground. Dropped, broken?

No, it works.

Holy God, that was a close one. Clouds of dust and smoke . . .

———————

Orpheus, Descending

Someone must go through that door.

Someone *must* go through that door.

Go through that door, Harry, and there

    will be no turning back.

Even if you did, you would never be the same.

Want to know what's through that door, Harry?

Let me ask you a different question:

What if this war goes on forever?

What if the war never ends?

What if fighting is all that there is?

What if killing becomes a new god?

What then?

Still want to know what's through that door, Harry?

Then go and look . . .

And he does.

Something switches inside his head.

I didn't make him, I swear, not me.

He chose to go through that door,

and take Agatha with him too.

As they crouched in the shelter,

the deep Camden shelter,

a rocket bomb struck the pavement directly above,

shaking the ground, shaking their nerve.

The German girl said, Harry, I'm scared,

and Harry took her cold, slender hand,

that hand of poor circulation,

as clouds of dust flooded into their cave.

Billowing black smoke bringing

Pandemonium.

Harry took one long look around,

then opened the door that would take them

much

farther

down.

Farther

down.

Towards

doomsday.

Imagine this:

The war goes on forever. It doesn't stop. Men keep
    fighting and dying while others keep making
    devices to help them do those things.

Smarter and quicker.

Stronger, deadlier.

Scientists creating new forms of death.

Explosions are one thing

but they're so messy and loud;

what about unseen, invisible clouds

that can kill with radiation

or with chemistry?

Or bacteria.

That's a Greek word, and I, Orpheus, hang my head.

What about weapons made from the atom?

That's Greek too: it means *indivisible*.

But what if it *could* be split into two?

Do you know what would happen?

Have you any idea of the horrible power

that would come from within?

What about robots smaller than dust

that swarm in a cloud and enter your lungs,

enter your bloodstream and enter your brain?

They could be made to eat you, from inside out;

they could be made to control you

and turn on your friend.

That's what you get when the war doesn't end.

All of this waits for Orpheus Black,

even now.

Watch.

Harry and Agatha stumble through the blackness.

The beam of their flashlight feeble in the gloom.

And with every step, the noise gets louder;

that dreadful hum from underground.

Louder and louder with every step,

as closer they come to the source of the sound.

What is it, Harry?

What is it?

Are you sure you want to know?

———————————

December 31 (?), Early morning
Underground

Feel like I'm blundering around. As usual! Not sure quite where we are. We took a long, long drag down the access tunnel from the deep shelter, the burning black smoke from the rocket strike pushing us farther and farther. My head felt really queer, a stabbing pain, and then it was like that big space was opening up in it again. Very dark beyond the no access door; all kinds of hell was breaking loose around us or overhead. You'd have thought they would have run out of the things by now, not much left to throw at us, but it seems they have a never-ending supply, these unseen attackers of ours . . .

In the darkness my vision jumped with stars, thousands of tiny points of light swirling, and I had to sit down for a moment; I remember Agatha bending down and taking my hand and being very kind, but very firm.

Then the bloody flashlight went out.

Perhaps that's why it had been left, all but dead.

I admit I started to panic, but Agatha sat down next to me and said something like: You have no choice. You have to keep going. And then she smiled and said, Come on, Orpheus.

A joke at a moment like that!

Harry, I reminded her.

She waved a hand. *Ach,* names!

She's so calm. When you think about the anti-Semitic bilge you hear day in, day out. When they spread rumors about the stampede at Bethnal Green last year being the fault of panicking Jews. And this young girl is so composed.

Ignorance = the worst enemy of all.

Bit of a blank after that. I remember we fumbled into a flight of stairs, really old ones, and we were climbing down and down for what felt like half an hour, but couldn't have been. Some kind of interlinked basements chock-full of rubbish, and we had a rest, found some tins of sardines, and I wolfed them down. Hadn't eaten anything as far as I can remember since the brussels sprouts. Is that possible? I'd normally be a basket case without food. Must be the shock, medicine, anxiety about Ellis, all keeping me going.

After that we squeezed down a tiny brick-lined corridor, filled with rubble from some blast, and came to this place.

Steps down again, but the whole of this subterranean space is flooded. Fireman in me says it must be an improvised fire tank, or else maybe one of the reservoirs has ruptured nearby and drowned this place. Gray light seeping down is almost worse than no light at all, but at least I can see to write this and take stock. Water's dark and cold and smelly, and it's hard to make out what kind of stuff is floating around in it. Keeping my new ritual, I lobbed a blue eye into the deep, and it made one of those plops that tells you a pool's very, very deep. (And this time, the eye didn't see anything at all.)

Dead end really, as I don't think either of us fancies the swim. But when I suggested to A that we turn round and go back, this look of absolute horror filled her face.

Me: We'll just retrace our steps. Smoke will have cleared from the Camden shelter now.

To which Agatha said loudly, as loudly as she's spoken yet: We can't. I can't go back. NO.

As if something back there is worse than what's ahead of us. I felt gooseflesh prick my skin.

Why? What's so bad about that? I said, a bit impatient. I need to get to Ellis and this is a cul-de-sac. A dead end.

I nearly lost you, Agatha said, quietly now, her calm returning. I cannot lose you now.

Do you mean in the smoke? I said.

No. You looked awful, she said. I thought you were dying. You can't die on me, Harry. Not yet.

That got to me, I can tell you.

Thought I picked up that humming sound a few minutes ago, but I can't hear it now. Every now and then there's a fizzing, like electrical stuff shorting out, and a little burst of light. Dr. Caligari or Nosferatu wouldn't be out of place down here. It's like an expressionist film set. Well, Fritz Lang did invent the countdown for rockets after all. Bit of smoke, electrical burning. Water stinks. Not sure even a sewer rat would want to swim through that.

I can hear something now. Something in the water? And there's something bigger across the far side, a glimmer of light now, maybe a lantern.

Oh, but my head is damn well killing me.

A boat on the water . . .

————————

Charon

I watched him pole across the water.

What do they say?

I remember it like it was yesterday.

And yes,

I've been to the Underworld countless times

as I've lived through other people's lives,

but this was the first time,

and I wasn't so brave;

and, listen, it was *my wife*

that I was trying to save.

Bitten by a snake on her wedding day,

and carried away.

Carried down, to the Underworld,

and when she died I lost everything;

I even lost the will to sing.

For months I mourned her, hollow and bare;

my misery mounted and threatened to kill me;

till finally I knew there was but one thing to do.

To descend to the Underworld and bring her back.

Naked, I smeared gypsum on my skin.
From head to toe I recast myself
in white, as one of the dead.
A ghost.
A near-forgotten soul,
I took my cape and my lyre
and made my way to the mouth of the cave.

I ventured in.
No hesitation;
I'd come to do what I was born to do,
to be what I was born to be,
to see my love affair to the very end,
even should that mean the end of me.
So,
I ventured underground.

As if it were yesterday, I remember
how I came to the edge of the still black water,
and, wondering how I should be able to cross,
the sound of splashing came to my ears.
Charon. The Boatman, come to collect.
His long low boat slid into the sand
and he held me with a steady gaze; and
as he watched me, I watched him,
he who, oh so recently, ferried my wife
across the Styx and thus ended her life.

He held out his hand, asking for payment.
I said not a word. I pulled out my lyre
and began to sing. Of love, and loss,
of our wedding day,
of how my wife was taken away;
and then amongst millions
I saw he remembered my bride,
and then, saying nothing,
stepped aside.

So, I made the journey.

Of how it turned out, I don't wish to speak. Not now. I

   told you before: a little triumph, a little tragedy.

That was my time, so long ago.

Now it's Harry's.

Will he go?

Will you go, Harry?

Harry,

will you cross the water?

You, and your adopted daughter?

Remember what I told you in my song,

and know that lives are not so long.

But once you head down this tumbling track,

Harry, believe me, you cannot turn back.

———————————

December 31 (possibly), Dawn

We're sitting on wasteland in thin light. It looks all of a piece when you've seen as much as I have these last twelve months, and smoke and fog are shrouding everything.

I feel like I've been away from myself. (Father would say impatiently, *What the hell does that mean, Harry? You need to wake up, boy!*)

Well, I am awake now. And I am here, wherever here is. Around us is the usual tumble of masonry and beams, and amongst it all the dislocated objects of everyday civilized life: slippers and saucepans and books and a charred Christmas tree. Bells clanging in the distance as the fire and ambulance services sort out the chaos left by last night, a long, drawn-out howl of the all-clear.

In short: the usual bloody mess. The rockets and so forth keep rearranging the deeply familiar and making it utterly unfamiliar. There's a church in the fog that I feel I ought to recognize, but it's surrounded by piles of rubble, and even the

street has turned into a winding path like the track that animals would cut on a rocky hillside.

But I wasn't *here* for a bit. I was somewhere else. Sod it, head feels weird. Agatha and I were trying to cross that water, weren't we? Weren't we . . . I know this sounds crazy . . . underground?

God, I can't remember. I'm suddenly terrified I'm losing my marbles. That I dreamed the whole thing about the dark water, but it's so hard to be sure. Everything is so disjointed. I can't keep asking Agatha what I'm doing. I'm the adult; I should be making sure she's OK, not the other way about. But everything is so confused.

That story Oakley told me in the Royal Free comes back. How he nearly floated up and *over the bloody rainbow.* That phrase made me smile in the hospital bed, a weird mix of Judy Garland and Oakley's solid language, but now the whole tale seems more real. That's how I feel now, like I've been floating around somewhere for the last few hours, inhabiting some other kind of world—and only now have I come back to my senses. Literally. Looking at the last entry in this notebook. A *boat*? Was that an idea for *Warriors*? A dream?

Well, first job is to find out where we are and get to the White Horse; it'll be easier in the light. I'll have another go at digging for Ellis, and then, whatever happens, help Agatha. Then it may be a good idea if I check back in with that worried-looking doctor at the Royal Free, just in case I'm not quite all there.

Agatha looks keen to get going. She said she knows where she is now and that she recognizes the ruined church.

Me: You mean this is where you were living? Where are we, then?

Agatha: I just know we need to go right, Harry, then left.

Me: To find your parents?

The White Horse

You're confused, Harry.
Don't you realize where you are?
You have made the first step,
and that's far.
But I feel the confusion in your head;
I see the way you're shaking with fear.
You think you've lost me, but I'm still here.
I'm with you, in you, every step of the way,
as you're walking through the damaged day,
taking Agatha by the hand.

And there's one thing, Harry, you know for sure.
Your brother needs you,
as much as this girl,
as much as he *always* needed you,
and there's a journey to be made.
But I sense you need some help, some aid,
So let me steer your stuttering steps,
put you on the proper path.
Come, Harry, and follow my lead;

I'll put you where you want to be;

for the journey takes you

here:

the White Horse.

This is where you need to be,

and there's a man you need to see.

His name is Greene.

You knew him once;

a lifetime ago, in days gone by

before the bombs fell from the sky

and left you like this:

a shattered and empty man.

Go to him, Harry,

see him! Speak!

Do not believe that you're too weak.

There's surely life in the old dog yet.

I believe in you, Harry: I know you're strong,

but you've still to learn the power of song.

And when you do, you'll know like me

that song can truly set you free.

———————

New Year's Eve, Late afternoon
White Horse bomb site

Back to the blooming beginning again, like that bus driver said. We're sitting on the lip of the crater left by the V-2, and the smoke and fog have cleared to show us the full horror of the impact on the pub.

But even with the daylight, it's no bloody good. Worse somehow to see starkly how very hopeless our task is.

Agatha led me across town this morning, sure somehow of her route, past smoking piles of ruined lives, through streets that look almost like normal just a few yards away. I don't think I'll ever get used to that transition, the way you find a row of solid houses, and then that blank of a cleared site from '41 or the Little Blitz, just a rubbed-out space as if I'd taken a putty eraser to a charcoal drawing and left a blurred pale nothingness. Or the more recent transitions to blackened and charred chaos. These doodlebugs and their supersonic companions take a house and lift it up, muddle all the bits, then dump them back down, burnt and broken in a thousand pieces, and trapped in there somewhere are possessions and bodies and pasts and potential futures. Lines of people sifting, truck cranes cranking up fallen beams, the blank wet sky overhead oblivious.

I was tired, but it must have been Agatha's determination that led me on as we plowed across Finchley Road, got a cup of tea in a fugged-up café, windows running with condensation, to steady ourselves, and arrived back here as feeble sunshine started to spill down on the dying hours of the year.

It was an otherworldly scene, with a handful of figures standing like specters in the cold, veiled light. I expected a full-out effort to finish excavating the rocket site, but nothing much was happening. The few people around were like the lonely figures you see walking down to the sea or a river at the start or end of a day, gazing at the water for answers to questions they haven't really worded properly. Nothing to be done but stare at the horizon.

To one side, miraculously in one piece it seemed, the pub piano.

As soon as we reached the site, my energy returned. I threw myself down into the pit, wading through the remains, pulling at the bricks with my hands, trying to figure out where I dropped that eyeball, going at it like a madman with Agatha doing sterling work beside me.

I told her it might not be safe, but she just shook her head and kept toiling away.

I feel responsible for you, I said. You're only just out of the hospital yourself.

It is fine, she muttered. I promised you we would help each other.

If anything, the crater seemed deeper than before, the rim of it way up above us, as if the whole thing had sunk since I was last here, the heavy ruins dropping into a void of some kind below.

Then I heard someone shouting my name over and over. It was Greene.

He clambered down through the rubbish, shaking his head, telling me there was *no bloody point, lad.* That it wasn't safe and that even if E had been trapped, with this cold and no food or water, he'd be a goner by now.

Think of the blast damage alone, Greene said. I thought the whole bloody world had ended when that one came down! And why the hell aren't you in the hospital?

I ignored him and kept pulling at the dust and debris with my fingers.

It's not safe, he said again. We've shouted and listened, and they had dogs on it. There's no one down there, Harry. I'm sorry.

I told him I didn't believe it, and Agatha turned to Greene and said — so solemnly and carefully it almost made me laugh — I do not bloody believe it either.

And who do you think you are, young lady? Greene said, with one of those smiles of his. Queen of bloody Sheba?

I am helping Harry, she replied, jaw set in determination. God bless her.

That's the ticket, Agatha, I said. Let's keep digging.

Greene shrugged and said to *blooming help yourselves* and walked away.

Agatha and I kept up a steady effort, moving a few more barrowfuls of brick and timber—and then, marvelously, a few minutes later Greene came back down into the crater again, with a shovel and a crowbar, and without a word rolled up his sleeves and got those big forearms of his working, the blurred tattoo of a snake there moving over the sinews.

Thanks, I said, after another handful of minutes.

Can't leave it to a girl—and a bloody conchie! he said with a wink, and we kept digging and digging as the last of the year ran out.

For a while it felt like we were making progress. Hauled some big timbers out and managed to crawl under a whacking big column of some kind into a cold pocket of air beneath. Encouraging to know breathing spaces exist down there. Every now and then, we stopped and I called again and listened, heart thudding away, straining to hear for anything, a tapping maybe, or a cry.

But there was nothing.

Come on, lad, Greene said, wiping sweat off his forehead, face lined by the effort. Give it up. There's nothing. And they're going to fill it in later today anyway. Stabilize it, the council man said. Come on. I'll bring you a sandwich from home. I've got some bacon for the first time in weeks!

I said Agatha would need something other than bacon, but she just smiled and said she wasn't really hungry.

You've got to eat, love, I said. Keep your strength up. (She hasn't had anything since we left the hospital.)

I'll see what I can rustle up, Greene said. (There is kindness as much as cruelty, even now. And when we work out how to brush away the ignorance, you can only hope that it will bloom even harder, like a plant cut back hard responds in the spring.)

Greene climbed out, but still I couldn't stop. The sight of the void beneath that pillar had given me fresh hope to go with the desperation, and for a good while longer I kept clawing away at anything that would shift, chipping nails, snagging the skin on my hands. All the time Agatha kept pace, breathing hard, glancing at me when she moved a decent chunk to show what she'd done and fire me on.

But there were no more big spaces to crawl into, just crushed-up brick and dust, all compacted tight. I felt my newfound sense of hope floundering, felt the return of fear and dread stealing through my veins. I pushed them away as firmly as I could, and kept burrowing like Ellis's fox, that animal pull to get underground overwhelming my body again even though my head was telling me it was useless.

In the end I only stopped when I saw Agatha slump down exhausted on a mound of rubble beside me. She looked even paler than normal. That brought me back to my senses with a slap, and at last I felt my own exhaustion, the nagging throb in my scalp.

I *must* look after Agatha. Can't let anything happen to this girl before I somehow reunite her with her parents.

I've got my wind back now, and again, despite the return of despair, I have the nagging feeling that the game isn't up yet. It's like I can *feel* Ellis somewhere close by, the kind of sensation I used to get when we played hide-and-seek in the woods and the hairs on the back of my neck told me he was creeping up on me from behind. Problem is now, maybe that sensation's just a product of the concussion and morphine and whatever else they pumped into me.

Sod it, maybe I'm just losing it. Maybe food will help us both. We're waiting for that sandwich, cold, tired—and very hungry. Agatha has wandered over to the rescued piano and is pecking away at the keys, some of them ringing out across the bomb site, some of them just making dead, percussive thumps. Think she must be good on a decent instrument, the way she sits there, the way her long fingers chase each other over the ivory and ebony. She looks the part.

———————

Horde

Harry! Look out!
There are demons here!
A horde of monsters in human form,
like vultures scenting the weak and bleeding;
they're heading for you,
you and the girl.

Oh, they come wheeling in,
flailing and screeching,
and even their voices are like nails across slate,
so filled they are with hate.

Don't misunderstand me.
I am not a saint.
I am no better than anyone
alive or dead.
I've had my share of anger;
I've been afraid,
frustrated
and I've uttered words of hate,

but these are things behind me now

and I can tell you when they went.

I left them behind when I went underground.

The things I saw there:

the suffering, the pain,

the blood pouring like rain,

the torments and anguish.

Unspeakable.

It was unspeakable.

And all the result of men and women who lived their lives

carrying one terrible thing inside themselves.

Hate.

Strange.

Like a bundle of ice on a throbbing wound,

the sights I saw in Hell were a salve to my own anger,

and I swore I would never hate again. Just sing.

Sing.

And now my song is loud!

Look out, Harry!

Look out!

They're coming!

———————————

Later, still at the side of the crater

Well, that was a rum do and a half. If I was cold before, now my blood's up, running hot.

A crowd of women gathered round me as I drew, like people tend to. I don't mind normally, but thought I recognized some of them from the pub the other night—and now they were in a foul mood. Angry from the start and looking to pick a fight. Agatha was still at the ivories, and she called out to me over the half a tune she was playing.

Harry, I am imagining the notes I cannot hear. Can you hear them?

The women closed tighter all around me, shoving, trying to wrestle this book out of my hands.

Whatcha doing? one shouted, jabbing her finger at the rough sketch map I'd made of where we'd been: the deep shelter, the bomb site, and the Royal Free all marked with X's.

I told them I was drawing.

Their leader, sharp face, cigarette in hand: Why? You a spy or something?

Made the mistake of saying I was an artist.

An artist? La-di-da! I tell you what you are. A ponce.

I assured them I wasn't and would they kindly leave me alone as I'd just lost someone. I pointed at the bandage on my head for good measure, hoping that would somehow help.

Heavyset woman: Why aren't you fighting, love? You can see what them Jerries are doing to us.

I expect most of *them Jerries* are as bloody well fed up with this as we are, I said, too prickly for my own good. As usual.

And then, for some reason, Agatha picked that moment to utter her first words of German since we left the Royal Free. Harry, *möchtest du ein Duo mit mir spielen?* Would you like to play a duet with me?

Bloody Kraut, one of the women hissed, turning towards A. My darling Frank was killed at bloody Dunkirk, you little bitch. By your lot.

Now I saw red. Leave her alone. She's a Jew; she and her parents have fled Germany, you stupid woman.

A conchie and a Yid, the leader of the ragged women sneered, fumbling for half-remembered words. Agents provocatives, that's what you are. Fifth columnists I'll be bound, reporting back to help guide your bloody rockets better. I'm getting the law.

No, said another. I'll fetch Jimmy and his mates. We'll sort it ourselves. Like that other one.

Agatha, bless her, she didn't hear or understand—or even seem to recognize the problem. I couldn't see her now, just hear her; she kept playing, the tune with its gaps and buzzes flying out from under her fingers. Shifting from something that could have been Schumann to something else, something that felt very familiar indeed.

All the time I could hear Agatha playing—and suddenly a kind of miracle happened: the tune flowered under her hands. It's hard to put it into words, but it was as if all the missing notes didn't matter, and the melody soared and changed pace, notes flying from the broken instrument, lively and uplifting and somehow smudging out the ugly words and anger in the air.

The women hesitated, parted, turned towards Agatha, and for an awful moment I thought they were going to attack her.

And then I saw him. A young man, tall and slim, had parked himself on the beer crates next to A and was playing the treble part of a duet, his head thrown back and hands moving fast, while Agatha, transported and smiling, made the bass notes rumble, and the whole effect was so beautiful and uncanny, it stopped everyone in their tracks.

The tune tumbled from their fingers: it made me think of the
hillside back home again, everything moving, clouds over Foxes
Hill, the wind in the trees, the cascading stream. And suddenly I
had the clearest, sharpest of memories that lifted my spirits from
the hopeless task behind me as I watched the young man next to
Agatha. I remembered a cold March day when Ellis and I made
such a good job of the dam we were building in the stream that
rolled down between our garden and the farm beyond, that we
shifted the whole damn thing from out of its bed and sent it, glittering, silvering, snaking down the green grass of Grice's meadow and
flooding into his yard. We laughed, clapped our hands in glee, and

capered around watching the results of our handiwork, numb fingers forgotten. (And then got a thrashing from Father that, though fierce, failed to dampen our spirits.) I'd forgotten that: two brothers on the edge of springtime arm in arm, delighting in our liberation of the stream.

Oh, Ellis. What we achieved together! Could still do.

The women lost their thread somehow and turned to listen to that crazy duet, their words stilled in their throats until, after a long while, one of them just said *well* and then tailed off. A strange look in her eyes. The sun had slipped through the gray and was almost warm on our faces now, and Greene came shuffling back with two steaming sandwiches, helping to lift the mood even more. Bacon! And cheese for Agatha. Though she just shook her head, turned hers down. Glad to see she lifted the cup from the thermos of soup to her lips at least. Gave me a reassuring smile over the brim, as if to say, *There, you see, I am eating.*

This man, Greene said, turning to face the women and slapping me on the back at the same moment, is under my protection. Here, in what is left of my pub—the ground at least must still belong to me. Now, sling your hook.

And they did, dumbstruck not by Greene, I don't think, but by the joyful racket that Agatha had been making with the young man.

I thanked Greene, then wandered over to the piano to talk to the young man and offer him the rest of my sandwich.

He looked up at me, his face older than I had first thought, lines thickening around the eyes, the marks of both laughter and tears, I fancied, his fair hair untidy, unkempt. He gazed at me with steady blue eyes that reminded me instantly of the ones nestled in my pocket. Angular face, clear skin.

He shook my hand, a smile playing on his lips. No thanks, mate. I'm a vegetarian. If you can believe that!

Then a queer thing: he looked me straight in the eye and said, It's really good to meet you again. Or meet you properly at least.

Do I know you? I asked.

Not really. We almost met the other evening. I like your work. I saw some of it at your exhibition at the Slade.

That brought me up short. But that was in Oxford, I said. I don't see how you could know me.

Oh, I know a lot of people, he said with another smile. A lot of people who work with paint and music and words. I know your brother, for example. Now, there's a fine poet by any standard.

He turned to mutter something to Agatha that made her laugh.

Bewildered, I tapped him on the shoulder. We've never met, though, have we? How could you know about a student like me?

He turned back, that clear blue light bright in his eyes.

Like I said, we nearly met the other night. He lifted his arms, cradling an imaginary violin, and mimed the push and pull of his bow.

Then I recognized him—the fiddler I saw making the children dance, the same one from the Heurtebise factory.

You were there in Kilburn the other night, I said.

He nodded. Keeping an eye on you!

What was that? The tune you were playing?

My head was aching, trying to make sense of this odd conversation. All I could manage to ask, of all things, was what tune he'd been playing.

Just an old thing, he said. This was a variation of it we were doing on the piano here. Your friend's a clever girl; she caught on straightaway.

He stood up and cast a glance at the crater behind me. Have to keep playing, mate, he said, whatever happens. Am I right?

Do you really know Ellis? I asked. I think he's under all that lot somewhere.

My voice cracked then, and I had to struggle to hold myself together.

He patted my shoulder. It'll all be OK, he said, and then turned away.

I've got to go and play for someone, he called over his shoulder. Up near the Heath.

Something about him felt reassuring, hopeful, even if what he was saying didn't make complete sense. I didn't want him to go and threw out another question: You're not in uniform, are you an objector too?

Not really, he said, walking away with a wave. But I'm not going to fight anyone. See you again, I'm sure. Happy New Year!

Agatha watched him go, past the piles of brick, the swept heaps of glass from blown-out windows glittering like ice.

He is a good man, she said, sucking the tips of her hair. He told me this will all be over soon. He's going to ask around to see if anyone has seen my parents. Send them to me.

Night's falling now. Year ending. No point digging anymore, especially in the fading light. Greene is offering us a bunk for the night, and I think we'll take it. If Ellis is down there, whether he's dead or alive, I don't feel I can abandon him like that and make the trek out to the Hudsons' place. We'll stay close, and tomorrow we'll dig some more. At least a bit longer. Can't give up all those years of brotherhood just because logic's telling you it's no good. And I can't face the thought that we are parting from each other on the sour note of the last couple of years. There has to be more than this. There *has* to be.

New Year's Eve, Evening
Greene's house

We're tucked up and cozy, and despite the bleakness about Ellis, I'm glad of the warmth. Greene's wife set a roaring fire in the grate, and we all huddled round it, watching the flames dance. Christmas tree in the corner, its decorations hanging still and intact, hard to believe the destruction just a street or two away.

I roused my spirits a bit, as much for Greene and his family as for myself, and told them I should have lodged with them all along. The Hudsons are good to me, but it's a bit far out.

The landlord laughed, lifting one of his boys up, that snake on his arm flexing with the muscle.

I wouldn't have taken you then! An art student with no references and no uniform? It was only a week or so ago that your brother told me what a decent bloke you are.

Ellis said that? I mumbled some reply, caught off guard, and felt tears stinging.

Greene nodded. Oh yes. He was drunk at the bar. But he meant it. You can tell things like that in my job. Went on about how you would be a great artist one day.

Then he looked somber. God, he said, it's New Year's Eve. Normally my busiest night of the year. And look at me!

Now it's late, the fire down to glowing coals, Agatha asleep. I keep thinking of what Greene told me—*in vino veritas,* they say, but did Ellis really mean that?

Ellis.

People always joked or teased or marveled how close we were. Nothing could prize you two apart, uncles and aunts would say, as we returned from some daft and misguided and frequently imaginary adventure on the hills, in the rivers, blood- or mud-daubed. Spooked, elated. Even when we fought, it was more like a ritual, pummeling away under big skies, stuffing grass in each other's mouths, locked in different versions of the same damn story. Dreaming the same dreams on the same nights as if we were twins.

But there's always a gap, a fissure, where the world can get in and start to push you apart. Perceived (?) parental favoritism, the effect of a first girlfriend breaking our charmed world, different strengths, different weaknesses. And there has to be, of course: we are different people. What saddens me is how wide that gap has become. We disagree about so much now, and when we talk, I see that push-pull of what we share and what we just can't stand in each other. But I need him to be alive. I need him to *be*. And while there's a chance, I'm going to give it everything I can to find him.

———————————

The Fight

The fight broke out over nothing.

Just nothing, nothing at all.

But it felt like it was everything

that threatened to fall,

to destroy you both:

brothers, with wheeling fists,

on an April hillside.

For a long time forgotten by you both.

It was years ago, when you were boys:

maybe you squabbled over a toy;

maybe one of you said something mean.

It's not important anymore

what you hit each other for;

and anyway,

you do not remember it now.

But I do, Harry;

I can feel it still.

I can feel the blows raining down

as if it were me they were striking

(and I *mean* every word I say).

As if it were me

who slugged, and scrapped,

and kicked and spat,

as if I were your brother,

or something like that,

while spring came rolling on in . . .

and never missed a beat.

——————————

Later

Awake again after fragmented dreams, broken thoughts muddling up waking and sleeping and memory. Just a mess of images until the last dream, which felt so real, so important. Something from long ago, I think.

Just me awake in the house now—from the sound of it just me awake in the whole blasted city. No sirens, no bombs, no shouting. My muddled head has been weaving together ideas for *Warriors* with things I've seen with Fire Force 34. There were snakes escaping from the zoo in my dream, fleeing the cull they ordered in case of bomb damage to the reptile house, and that was getting mixed with the return of those vicious ladies, this time with a bunch of gangsters for company. And then some of the *Warriors of the Machine* ideas came flooding back, all that stuff about robotic killing machines as small as insects. A sky thick with radio-controlled attack robots, tiny rockets that could sniff out a target or even think for themselves . . .

There are owls hooting outside—more than one, a host of them, some close by and loud, some farther off like echoes. With the blackouts they've been coming into the city more and more, bringing the childhood countryside with them. I like that; it's comforting somehow that they are withstanding the war, at least. So many cats were put down at the start of the war in '39 that the mice and rats have had a productive few years. (Ellis told me when we were still talking properly, his poetic eye bright, twinkling, that there was a secret mass grave in southeast London for the murdered felines—and let that imagination of his off the leash, picturing tens of thousands of ghost cats on the loose, sliding white along fences and through the undergrowth.) But ghost cats only catch ghost mice, so now the owls, white, tawny, are having a grand time scavenging the bombed wastelands and parks, crisscrossing darkened London skies, dropping silently to take what they need. Do they notice the rockets, the bombs, the fires, as being out of the ordinary?

One owl really close now, *tu-whoo*ing loudly. Apart from that, nothing but the whisper of my pencil.

The last of the dreams won't dislodge itself from my head. It was more coherent, more powerful, than the other bits and pieces: started with some kind of version of that memory of Ellis and me on the apple-green hillside, tricking the stream to flow somewhere else. But now we were in a house, something rather like our rambling childhood home, and we were on the stairs—neither young, nor old, just *us*—and somebody was clodding around on the boards overhead, making loud stomping footsteps like a giant in a fairy tale, and there was the sound of urgent, tumbling water. Voices too, muttered through the sound of the bath or toilet flush or rain overflowing the old gutters, and then suddenly the stairs were awash with a flood. Sheets of water lipping over each step one by one, falling towards me, and I looked round for Ellis, checking my older brother's reaction (like I invariably did back then) to see what my reaction should be—joy, wonder, fear?

But he was gone. And more than that, I sensed he was irrevocably gone, swept out of existence in that moment and now somewhere I could never reach. Or not quite.

I turned, knee-deep in the cascade, and looked down. The stairs jinked and twisted, once, twice, three times, and the water kept tumbling, through a hole in the floor of the hall, down into some kind of gaping basement, engulfed by the darkness. Somebody—it might have been Agatha, but I only saw her hand—gave me a flashlight, and though the beam wasn't strong, it shone through the falling water into the darkness and, briefly, illuminated Ellis's face. He was gazing up at me, reaching out a hand. And then I heard Oakley's voice quite distinctly, as if he were standing at my shoulder, saying, *It's OK, it's just a matter of braving the blooming water. Get a move on, you daft bugger!* And I started to wade down the slippery stairs, gripping the banister, knowing it wasn't too late, knowing that if I was fast enough and brave enough, I could still save Ellis.

I woke abruptly.

And now I'm more sure than ever that Ellis isn't done yet. He's down there somewhere. I've just got to find a way in. Not impossible, after all. I've come across it enough myself: people pulled from the wreckage of a terrace reduced to carbonized nothingness, and all they've got is a raging thirst. One chap, gruff old codger we dragged back into the light in Islington, grabbed my hand and ran his tongue across his cracked lips. I thought he was about to thank me or ask about a relative, but he just coughed up the words: *And what took you so bloody long?*

It's not just the images in the dream, but the feeling of urgency. I'm sure he's not lost yet. Or maybe my head's just worse than I thought, and something fell into it through that crack in the skull and is busy making up stories, getting things muddled. (Too much imagination's dangerous, boys, Father always told us. And we nodded, and then secretly let ours off the leash.)

Greene and his wife have been so kind to us, but I have to go.

Agatha's asleep soundly now in the camp bed they've made up for her. Maybe I should leave her to this family's resources and decency, at least for the rest of this night. I'm a mess right now. Her breathing is so calm again, her face relaxed and that photo propped next to her.

I'll let her recover here for a bit—didn't like that exhaustion on her face when we were digging—and come back for her later tomorrow when I've satisfied myself about Ellis one way or the other. I'll leave her a note—and an eyeball for Greene and his family on the dresser.

And then I'll go.

Spring

Somewhere,

on the other side of the world

(probably),

there's a tree that no one has ever seen.

I don't know where it is.

I don't know what it's like.

It could be small; it could be mighty.

It could even touch the sky.

I don't know; no one does.

But,

I do know this:

its arms are laden with insects

that are not yet named.

Beneath its boughs stalk other beasts,

who as yet have not been tamed.

Around its trunk twine tendrils

of plants of unknown green,

and in the ground beneath its feet

crawl creatures never seen.

No one must know this tree;

I hope they never do.

It's vital that there remains a place

far from the reach of me, and you.

Far

from there

lies London.

Nineteen hundred and forty-four.

Where,

walking through the city,

it's easy to feel

that the whole world is a ruin

of rubble and twisted steel.

A planet of desolation,

of rolling dust and smoke,

of poisonous air that cannot be breathed;

even the sun is choked.

And what is this destruction for?

There has to be a why,

there has to be a reason,

to pull the sun out of the sky.

I love mankind,

I truly do.

I think of all the things we've done that are beautiful and true.

But then I think of other things,

like guns and hand grenades,

like armored tanks and rocket bombs,

that the mind of man has made.

And then it becomes hard to sing,

much too hard to sing.

So.

What's it for?

What is all this destruction for?

We're making a new world,

I heard someone say

as I walked through Vauxhall the other day.

In Dalston I saw someone shake their head

and mutter,

If this is life, I'd rather be dead.

In Balham I saw two children run

at the sound of a buzz bomb overhead;

and when it was done they said not a word,

for the simple reason that they were dead.

From Clapham to Dresden,

from Hamburg to Bow, I hear

people ask, Why? I have to know!

All of them with the same question as mine,

and answers are so hard to find.

For Justice! For Vengeance!

Some even say *Peace!*

But are these solutions?

I cannot tell,

and yesterday I heard this:

— bomb them to Hell.

Those were the words

of a vicar in Hampstead.

I did not dwell to hear more.

I walked on.

Trying to find a familiar song,

trying to find a seed of hope.

And then I saw it

and knew.

I did not need a metaphor,

for what I saw was this:

a weed. Just a weed,

pushing its way through piles of broken bricks,

and then I knew

that yes, perhaps,

we are making a new world;

and when we're done,

nature will make a gentler one.

———————————————

New Year's Day, Morning,
wasteground. Lost

The light is returning and we've stopped for a rest after our trek through the rubble. I say "we" because Agatha—bless her!—is still with me.

Trying to be as silent as possible, I'd got no farther than Greene's front door when I must have made some kind of noise, and she opened her eyes and sat up, wide awake in a moment, and standing resolutely with me and taking my hand in the next. She looked me in the eye and said, *I am coming with you. Harry. No arguing. It's our fate.*

And here we are. We should accept the people fate brings into our lives and love them with all our heart, a wise man once said. So . . .

I thought we'd go back to the far side of the bomb site, try and poke around in neighboring exposed cellars to see if I might work my way under the crater. But somehow—ridiculously—we've managed to lose our way and ended up in a real muddle,

walking for ages. That's the trouble after the big raids: everything is transformed, landmarks obliterated overnight. Add to that the partial blackout and Bob's your uncle. We're lost. What a way to start the year!

I've never seen the streets so empty—even when the evacuations happened in '39, or after the big raids of '41. For an hour or two, Agatha and I didn't see a soul. The fog thickened, thinned, then *really* thickened back into that old sheep's wool again, and we were well and truly disorientated. I began to think I'd made a mistake leaving Greene's warm and cozy house, and perhaps something got to A too, because, rounding a corner and seeing the mountains of rubble in front of us, the burnt-out brick and steel and wood, she reached out a hand looking for mine.

It felt cold. I squeezed it back. Didn't want to alarm her, but didn't want to lose time now.

Agatha, I said, as calmly as I could, have you any idea where we are?

A frown on her face. Why?

Me, forcing a smile: I think I've lost my way.

This is near where I was living, she said quietly, pointing at the blast-damaged block in front of us, hazy in the dust and smoke and half-light. I think I recognize that building.

You're sure? I asked. So do you think your parents might be close by?

And then it all got stranger. She frowned again. No, Harry. Now I do not think they are here, she said. I do not think they make the journey in the end.

I asked her what she meant by that, but she just gave me the saddest smile I have ever seen and shook her head. Looked away.

I told her that I didn't understand, that I must have got myself in a muddle.

It is my fault, she said bravely. It is very hard to explain.

When we find someone around here, I'll ask. Head's feeling really odd again and knees a bit weak. Perhaps I'll rest awhile and get Agatha to scout ahead and find someone to ask exactly where we are. Need to calm myself, but I keep feeling the urgency of that falling water and the staircase, the drop into the cellar or whatever darkness lay below.

———————————

Sisyphus

Rock roller
push boulder
timeless torture
under ground.

Back breaker
inch stealer
take your punishment
make no sound.

Roll your rock to the top of the ridge
inch by inch
hour by hour
day by day
year by year.
Roll your rock to the top and then,
watch it roll back down again.

This is not the place to speak of your crimes, Sisyphus.
This is the place to speak of your punishment.
Staggering step after staggering step
up that hill, eternally
pushing that boulder before you;
figure of futility.

I remember I saw you when I was in Hell.
How you shuffled and lumbered, your back to the rock.
I asked who you were, and when they told me,
I watched for a while, to see if you'd stop.
O Sisyphus, how you keep on fighting
against your endless pointless pursuit;
you keep on making meaning from nothing,
then see that meaning be nothing again.
How do you do it?
How, and why?
What makes a man continue to try?
Is there a secret to your infinite toiling?
And do you know what it means to feel joy?

Only philosophers can offer us answers;

the rest of us try just trudging on.

Some aren't even aware of the question,

and I?

Well, I have my song.

Sisyphus.

Do you remember when I came before Hades;

did you stop for a moment to look?

Not for a second, no, not one:

you kept on working as I started to sing.

Kept on pushing, and pushing, but then

I sang to Hades and Persephone;

decanted my song, fluid and free;

let each word take them,

let each note make them,

wrap them and trap them and fill up their hearts,

till they started to sob as they sat on their thrones.

And as I finished, then I saw

another miracle,

one of your own:

you sitting still upon your stone.

Sisyphus, I thought of you today.
Here, in the wasteland of London.
This man called Harry, this *Orpheus* Black,
and Agatha;
these wanderers amongst the rocks
came to a patch of open ground,
where in huddled ones and twos
hunched-up figures bent to a task
that reminded me
of you.

Scratching and scraping,
sifting through rubble,
hunting for things of worth.
Endlessly searching,
rolling and lifting,
clearing the ruins of last night's attack.
Making only the smallest difference
till the bombs of tonight bring it back.

What are they looking for?
Why do they do it?
Broken and bent and beaten down,

scavenging for nothing,

for nothing seems to be found,

just the endless toil of clearing the ground.

Harry approached them,

asking aloud,

Who's in charge here,

and what are you doing,

and can you help us find a way down?

Their leader,

a man of uncountable years,

straightened his back and came face-to-face;

stubbed his finger on Harry's coat,

and spoke.

Leave us alone. You've no business here;

nothing we're doing is wrong.

And then: something else I hadn't predicted;

Harry gave them a song.

In the face of that anger, he took a step back,

he opened his mouth and music came out.

This man from the Marches, who claims not to sing,

tipped up his head and let it ring.

I stood in wonder, I listened with awe,

as the girl joined in and helped with the tune.

I stood and stared as if at the moon.

I, whose life was *created* through song,

I, who tamed the wildest of beasts,

had never seen it in quite the same way;

as *someone else* wove wondrous sounds,

it was all I could do to stay on my feet,

and laugh as the hunched-up ones and twos

stopped their work and crowded around,

and listened to Harry and clapped their hands,

laughing and smiling; and so for a time

they forgot their punishment,

forgot their crime.

And when it was over,

with flickering smile,

their leader took Harry in hand

and said, D'you understand,

you've given us a wonderful gift,

a song from nowhere to lighten our load.

So I must give you a gift in return,

something to take on your road.

Harry pointed at the ground.

That, he said. A way down.

That's what I want;

and the man said, *Sir,*

why don't you look around?

Can't you tell?

To me it seems we're already in Hell;

to go only deeper is madness itself,

so what can I give you to take on your way?

He thought for a moment.

He looked at the girl.

Put dusty finger to grimy curl.

Here, he said, this is the thing.

This is who we're fighting for,

and understand this:

when I say fighting,

I don't mean war.

I'm speaking here of greater things

than Nazi leaders and British kings.

She's not your daughter, I can tell,

but I can see you love her well,

and so you should, for she is life:

she is deliverance from eternal strife;

she is pacifism; she is peace;
she's goodwill before the armistice.
Above all else, you know, it's true:
she is the feminine in you.

So spoke the man.
When he was done, he turned to the others, turned
    back to their toil, of shifting through the broken
    soil, left Harry to stare at his retreating back,
    who felt Agatha tug his hand and say,
Harry, I didn't understand.
His English was funny, don't you think?
Shall we sit by their fire before we go on?
Why are you crying?
Did I do something wrong?
No, said Harry, not you.
It's we who've done something terribly bad.
Not you. Not you.

Not you.

———————————

New Year's Day, Sunset

I've been asleep. Head full of the fog. Dogs barking in the distance. All around us the towering mounds of broken buildings like Gothic ruins.

The sun for once is a perfect disk. Orange and dulled by the dust in the air, the smoke from fires, the sun is setting for the first time this year. And next year? Does it go on like this? Suppose we win the war like Ellis says is inevitable. Then what? A respite and then just more of the same? No, it will keep changing, developing. Who expected the V-1s a year ago? And who could have dreamed up the rockets that come hurtling at us from the upper edges of the atmosphere? We are taking our machines to the edge of space, and when we look down, the world is going to seem very small. Very conquerable. Maybe we won't win it. Maybe the supersonic ray will wipe us clear off the Earth. Or maybe the humming sound, or whatever *our boys* are working on, will beat them to it and unleash something terrifying the other way.

Agatha is sitting, looking at the figures gathered round the fire a few yards away. I search the entry above this one, scour my memory, but can produce nothing but a blank. Nothing but the sketch of a man with a barrow full of rock, and the refrain of a song echoing around my vacant head.

More information, not that it helps, furnished by A. She found these people who told us they were working to clear this mountain of rubble by hand. Apparently they've been at it for *simply ages; never seems like there'll be an end to it,* one of them said to her. And this is where it gets even stranger still.

Agatha tells me I asked them where we were, if we were near the site of the White Horse, but they said they weren't sure. They just had to keep going. Told us to clear off in no uncertain terms.

Are people trapped? I asked, and their leader, an old man with a roughed-up face, told us there was a staircase down into the Underground here somewhere, and they felt they had to clear this place up. Nobody else seemed bothered.

Everyone seems to have forgotten about us, the man said. Every time the hole is almost clear, the excavated rubble slips and falls back in.

But you were amazing, Harry! Agatha said to me, her face lifting as she told the story. You began to help them and then started singing—that lovely tune—and after a while they all joined in, and everyone was singing together and working. Where did you learn to sing like that?

Bewildered, I told her I can't sing for toffee. Never could. Ellis was the chorister, the singer.

I think you sing very well, she said earnestly, looking puzzled and a bit concerned, and then trying to hide it. Can't you remember it, Harry?

I told her I didn't.

Agatha shrugged. Well. It happened. It was *sehr schön*. You looked so well and full of life, my Harry, my Orpheus.

I told her I didn't feel at all well. That I didn't want to let her down, that I didn't want to let Ellis down, but I was feeling useless.

You are not useless, she said. Not at all. I looked in your notebook again. It was beautiful. I hope you don't mind.

No, I said. But it's just a journal—me scribbling down stuff that seems to matter, first for my new project, then to try and keep my resolution. Now it's to gather my ideas together in case I forget stuff. I asked her if that made any sense and she nodded.

But it is more than that, she said. It is a very lovely diary. I liked reading about you finding me. You are writing very well.

I told her that was Ellis's department, but she just gave me that flash of a smile again and patted the back of my hand.

You must keep writing, she said. As much as you can. I think it is important. What is Warriors of the Machine?

It's just an idea I've been working on, I said. I told her that when I get back to the Slade Art School, I want to do a big illustrated book, with words and images combined; make a kind of warning. About how we're just going to become more efficient at killing each other unless we work out how to develop our better selves. Rambled on for a bit about killer robots and helmets that could control people from a long way away with radio waves or whatever.

It sounds very scary, Agatha said.

It is, I said.

Now the exhausted rubble heapers sit to one side, brewing tea in a blackened can over the bruised flame of a Primus stove, passing cigarettes, talking quietly amongst themselves. Words that don't convey anything but a shared burden, a brief respite. They look timeless as behind them the sun keeps slipping, darkening, going under.

Those dogs are getting louder. Angry-sounding things.

Time for an eyeball. I slip it into the dust that these people are making with their unceasing effort, and it catches that last bit of coppery light.

————————

Cerberus

———————

Harry, you're fading.

Fading, fast.

Any of your scribblings could now be your last.

But I can help you tell your tale.

When your words fail, I can help you speak.

I can walk inside you, when your legs are weak.

Can't you remember . . . ?

Those dogs?

Those wild, hunger-maddened dogs.

They come across the wasted ground.

Agatha: running, shouting.

One of the rubble sifters takes a burning firebrand;

throws it at the pack;

they scatter, but come back.

Snapping, snarling, biting, clawing,

and then another metamorphosis:

the dogs stop.

Raise their forepaws from the ground,

hips cracking, straightening backs,

joints twisting, muzzles receding,

fur falling, ears shortening,

as they become:

men.

Not just any men, Harry,

but the warriors of the machine.

X-Dogs of war. You looked into the future, Harry:

is this what you saw?

Men who don't know they're men anymore?

I, who can sense the smallest vibration

(for vibration is all that music is),

can hear that something is amiss:

the X-Dogs have helmets upon their heads,

helmets so cunning as can scarce be believed.

Trans-cranial subsonic manipulation:

sound waves control every thought and deed.

Direct stimulation of synapse and nerve

by subsonic waves crossing into the brain:

no more fear, no more dread, no more pain.

No more tiredness during a battle;

no more panic when danger's near:

fatigue removed and consciences cleared.

Man as machine, warrior dog:
who could have dreamed of such a horror,
who could have sat down and sold this to someone
and who could have placed it on another man's head?
Only the warriors, the warriors of the machine.

The dogs come closer; Harry steps back.
I can see in his eyes that he hasn't the strength,
and so I step inside him,
and sing.

We sing of things too lovely for words,
like children laughing and music dancing,
of apples and honey and grapes on the vine,
of the darkest red wine,
of the delight at the approach of spring,
of all the joy that love can bring,
of magical moments that happen in life:
like how, having climbed a hill,
you would still climb higher
and how eyes shine bright when we sit by the fire.
We sing of the pleasure of finding a word
for something unnamed before.

We sing of a thousand wonderful things,
then sing of a thousand more.

And then, Harry, look! Harry!
The dogs are removing their metal hats.
They stand as if they've just been born,
shaking their heads,
brushing webs of deceit from their minds,
and turn to each other,
smiling at first,
then laughing and joking
they turn towards the nearest man
and starting to dance, hand in hand,
shout, Orpheus! Orpheus!
You gave us your song,
stronger than anything nursing our brains;
found us and saved us and showed us a way
to stop. Just to stop and say,
I don't know you, but I love you like no other;
I love you like a brother.

———————————

New Year's Day. Nightfall

One of the dogs is curled at my feet. Her ferocity gone. The wolf has become a household faithful.

Agatha was really worried about me, but I feel better again now. In the gaps between whatever's happening to my head, I don't feel too bad. It's like listening to a faulty radio—the voice suddenly gone and drowned by static, but when it comes back, it's talking away as if nothing has happened and everything's fine.

The diggers are clearing the top of a flight of steps and have told me they think I'm close to where I need to be.

We're getting nearer, A said. I can feel it.

And I think I can too. I can sense we're on the right track again.

I push my hand into the fur at the dog's neck, outer layer trapping cold air, warm deeper down. She looks up at me now as I write. A different color, different size, of dog, but those eyes! She reminds me again so much of dear old Lottie, our childhood dog, one of the three pointers that Father had bought for shooting but became the family pet instead, so bad was she at finding and retrieving wounded or dead game. No interest at all in chasing falling, shot-filled ducks as they thumped down, feathers shredded. Just a joy in being alive — and keeping us all company. In the end she even warmed Father's heart after his initial frustration and disgust at her complete disinterest in training. Softened his grief a bit over Mutti when the rest of us couldn't do a thing to help him.

Lottie would roll over at the drop of a hat, tail wagging like anything, soft belly ready to be stroked. Or would beg Ellis and me to walk her on the wild tops of the hills. And we did. Miles and miles and miles of windy November days; clear mornings in May when you could look one way and see the flatlands of England stretched out in a haphazard green checkerboard, then look the other and see the sleeping mountains of Wales, summer evenings of slanting warm light. And always Lottie with us, snuffling, running rings around us, disappearing, returning. Quietly, secretly, we each thought of her as our own. And as she and we aged, I began to dread her passing more and more.

So when, hips giving out, deaf as the proverbial, Lottie started to have convulsions, we argued bitterly about what should be done. After one particularly horrific sequence of agitated aura, a prolonged fit of running legs and twisting neck, and then the long stumbling aftershock, things came to a head. To my astonishment Ellis sided with Father.

She's suffering. It's time we put her out of her misery. End of story.

I had assumed he would argue with me for a reprieve; I was taken aback. But even more so by the way he did it. Suddenly there was an Ellis I didn't know. Matter-of-fact. Harsh even.

No point being emotional about it. It has to be done.

And even though I knew he was right, I felt that gap open between us. As if he was already steeling himself for something worse to come.

I called him a coldhearted bastard, and he threw a punch at my head and caught me a glancing blow. Not the fights and arguments of childhood. Something grown-up and serious. Something with bitterness.

Long gone now, Lottie. Buried at the bottom of the sloping garden. But still I sense her walking with me sometimes.

Gateway

Hell is different for everyone.
And everyone finds their own way in.
This was another thing I learned as the years turned,
as leaves burned, as waters dried up,
as the ground roasted, as trees died,
as time and time again I made my way to the Underworld.

As we sat upon that blasted wasteland,
as the X-Dogs danced as merriful men,
Agatha turned and clung to Harry,
some sudden fear making her shake.
She sobbed into his side, saying,
Harry, O Harry, maybe they're dead.
It was all he could do to keep his head
and whisper her name and hold her hand,
and tell her things that it helped to hear,
that answers were near.

Harry was right.

As night came on,

the rubble sifters shifted more of London's ruins.

A mountain removed, brick by brick.

Underneath, thick wooden beams,

dragged away by tiring arms.

Then, the ground tilted.

Something slid.

They scrambled for safety

as a hole opened up,

revealing a downward-sloping ramp.

And there! At the end:

a staircase to the Underworld,

should any be brave to dare.

The sifters back away in horror;

the X-Dogs look, but don't approach.

Only Harry and Agatha come near,

climb down to the ramp,

head for the steps,

holding hands,

biting lips,

making wishes,

they turn to each other and force a smile.

This is the gate, Harry,

this is the stair.

Don't be scared by the putrid air.

Ignore the smell, and that terrible hum.

Forget that you ever saw the sun.

And standing there, Harry, you're telling yourself,

as you edge towards the lip of the ledge,

that this is the threshold,

your crossing place.

This, the moment you'll go underground.

Harry, oh, Harry, dependable friend,

it makes me weep to understand

you've no idea of truth anymore;

that *ever since* you heard my song

you've been in the Underworld

all along.

The staircase spirals down, Harry.

And yet you live, and life spirals up to meet you.

And Ellis? you ask. Does he still live?

The staircase

spirals

down.

———————————

Night, Underground, platform

We counted the steps till we lost track somewhere past two hundred and something. Dim emergency lights functioning, but only lighting a few feet of darkness around each bulb. Felt like we were penetrating some lost pharaoh's deep tomb, the broken bricks and masonry cluttering our descent at first, and then everything was calm, empty, and hushed. It felt good to be going down again; crazy as it sounds, it feels like this is the way to find Ellis and bring him back to the surface.

Agatha's clear eyes looked to me, trusting, encouraging me even, but still occasionally showing the wariness she must have had to live with before she and her parents escaped.

You don't have to come with me, I said, as we peered down into the gloomy well of the stairs.

She took a very deep breath. I do. You are guiding me to my parents.

Be reasonable, I said. They can't be down here, love. You

can wait up there, and I'll come back for you. Help you, as soon as I've found my brother.

She looked at me rather as you would an errant young dog. I'm coming with you. You are not well (pointing at my head), and you will get lost if I do not stay with you. And we will find my parents together.

We listened to the darkness, straining for the sound of voices or trains or—who knows—even that mysterious hum Ellis told me about what seems like weeks and weeks ago. Yet we heard nothing but our breathing, faint sounds from above of the rubble sifters getting back to work, and the slow crawl of distant planes.

I didn't recognize the stairwell. It was like the one at Covent Garden, but the tiled murals on the curving wall were strange to me. Bucolic scenes, dappled hillsides, pine trees, and magical creatures like fauns and centaurs picked out in olive, rose, lemon.

Don't suppose you know what station this is? I asked.

I didn't use the Underground before, Agatha said. But this reminds me of a station near our old house in Berlin.

She patted her pocket where she keeps that photo.

They'll be OK, I said.

Agatha nodded, bit her lip, peered down.

Footsteps were coming towards us, a slow trudge of boots

on the metal-shod stairs, ringing out in the gloom, and a pale light brightening the pictures on the wall that enfolded us. A minute later a heavyset man labored into view, breathing hard through his mouth, pausing now and then before climbing on another ten, fifteen steps and resting again, the tin ARP helmet shielding his face until he was nearly on us. When he looked up and his flashlight beam caught our faces, he almost jumped clean out of his skin.

He huffed, What the blazes are you doing down here? Wiped his forehead with a bloodred handkerchief.

Fire service, I said. Looking for someone. Putting as much authority into it as I could.

He looked me full in the eye. Well, I wouldn't go this way if I were you.

Why not? Agatha asked, stepping just that bit closer to me. The man's voice was thick with some anxiety, or disgust maybe.

Not safe. There's a collapse in the next tunnel down, might be gas or water leaks. And there's an old tramp down here, reckons it's his little empire. Bit unhinged, I think, off his head on something. They say he deserted at Dunkirk and swam half the way home. Rather violent if you catch him on the wrong day.

I told him we'd be just fine. After all it's probably just some poor misunderstood sod. They say some people came down into the Underground and shelters in '41 and have pretty much been down here ever since. Particularly the misfits, those who couldn't find a place or anything to belong to up there in the real world.

Well, I'm off duty now, the ARP man said, getting his breath back. For good.

Me: What do you mean?

ARP man: I've done my time. They're letting me go when the shift ends. Thank God. I shall sit in my allotment, and Jerry can keep bombing all he likes. I'm going to dig the soil in January and plant seeds and smoke my pipe and have a bumper harvest. Sweet peas for the missus. Happy New Year!

I told him it already was January by my reckoning and he laughed. New Year's Eve still, he said—a few hours left of this old year yet! I've been bombed out, but at least I still know what year I'm in! You must have got confused.

He laughed again, then thrust the heavy flashlight he was carrying into my hands. If you're going on down, he said, you'd better have this. Battery's brand-new. It gets very dark before it gets light again. Bomb damage even down here, and everything's a bit of a mess.

He looked us up and down. Well, cheerio. Watch out for Old Jimmy. He's got a few unpleasant so-and-sos working for him too. They guard him. Rough lot.

I thanked him, said I had nothing to pay him with after giving my last coins to Greene, and he said no matter.

Give him one of the eyes, Agatha whispered, and reached into my pocket before I'd had time to answer and slipped the man one of the eyeballs.

The man looked at it thoughtfully.

Very nice, he said. I'll put it on my windowsill in the shed. Thank you. Take care in the passages.

Then he climbed on up, feet banging away, echoes receding.

At the last I realized I'd forgotten to ask which station this was, and shouted after him, but he either didn't hear or was so out of breath that his reply was lost. I hope he'll make it through this last night on duty and then get to puff those clouds of blue-gray smoke across his ripening vegetables. The thought fills me with a kind of buoyancy again, the sense that we are doing the right thing.

Bit worried about how I keep flipping in and out, like I'm here one minute and gone the next. But Agatha seems a steady guide. We'll take it step-by-step. When I listen to the depths, I fancy I can hear that buzzing hum again. Just on the threshold of hearing, like a distant hive of bees, angry, muffled, on the way to swarm, but getting louder.

Still can't work out where I've gone wrong on the days, though.

Deeper underground, this year or next?

That ARP man must have been confused about the date. Or is it me? A pretty poor state when you don't even know what year it is! Don't know where we are. Don't know when we are.

We came down the mosaic-walled stairwell, through a doorway, and into a long echo of a corridor. Not a light on and glad to have the flashlight. We edged forward, thoughts of the ARP man's warning about Old Jimmy and his boys fresh on my mind. It's not that I worry so much about me; it's not letting Ellis down that matters. And also Agatha. Don't want to lead her into any trouble when she's got her parents looking for her. I told her again she should have stayed aboveground, kept safe up there, but she just grabbed my jacket sleeve and said again, I am coming with you. You are very important to me.

And again her smile lifted me, gave me new strength from somewhere.

Bless her.

The tunnel was wide, arched. We went forward, picking our way through scattered debris, a fallen pipe leaking wires. That smell of burning again and the hum louder. After about forty paces, I felt water drop onto my face, drip by drip, cold, refreshing, and the flashlight beam picked out what I can only describe as rain. A steady cold rain, percolating through the plaster overhead from some ruptured main or storm drain, falling the length of the tunnel, bringing the occasional chunk of white stuff away with it. More worried about keeping this damn book dry than myself. We dodged through it, stumbling, the tunnel extending for what felt like hundreds of yards, but I suppose was no more than the length of a platform, and came to a heavy door at the far end. No markings, no signs, no Keep Out. Just a heavy black door, open a fraction, the hum louder beyond, and a hint of smoke.

And then we heard footsteps ringing out behind us.

An angry voice: Oi, you two. Where do you think you're bleeding going?

I trained the flashlight behind us into the dark to show a tall man, dark coat flaring as he chased through the rain behind us.

I shouted I was looking for someone, that he was down here somewhere.

If you're after the boss, forget it, the man barked. He's deeper down. Have you brought anything for him? If you don't give Old Jimmy something, he'll not take kindly to that.

Now I saw the gun in the man's hand and pulled Agatha round behind me to shield her.

He waved the thing at me, closing the gap fast.

Just stand still, mate. And your little tart. Can't have any Tom, Dick, or Harry running around down here. Might see something you shouldn't. This is Jimmy's little empire, and we decide who goes where.

I told him to mind his language. That Agatha was a refugee, and she didn't need the likes of him chucking words like that about.

The man growled back at me, a sound full of derision, disgust.

I know one when I see one, mate. I can sniff 'em out. You don't get decent buggers looking for Old Jimmy. Just the likes of you and me. The likes of her.

That kind of thing.

What got me was the tone—hard, flint hard—and the way he kept the gun pointing at us as he stalked forward, jabbing it to underline each word, as if he knew everything about us. But he hadn't a clue.

I told him to put the bloody thing down. Seemed senseless having some kind of petty gangland spat down here in the middle of all the carnage.

He spat out a gob of phlegm. And who the hell are you, matey, to tell me what to do? he shouted. Nobody else can hear you this deep. You do as I say, or I'll drop you on the bloody spot. Perhaps I'll start with whatever you're carrying on you: cash, watch, coupons, ciggies maybe. He gestured with the black bore of the gun: Now *that* looks like a nice bit of gold on your girl's finger there. I'll have that for starters.

For a moment I thought I was shivering, from cold, perhaps even fear, though I didn't feel it, just a growing anger — rage — with this stupid man, what he was saying. Then I realized it was Agatha who was shaking, pressed tight behind me, trembling, her teeth chattering.

Don't let him take it, she whispered through the shivering. The ring belongs to my mother. I must not let it go, Harry. I promised Mutti I would keep it safe for her. Forever and ever.

The stranger's voice cutting over hers: You got any other jewelry, sweetheart? Lovely-looking thing like you must have.

My head was hurting again, blurring. I reached for A's hand, gave it a squeeze. Hadn't noticed the ring there before, but now it looked so obvious. Valuable.

I kept it safe all this way, she hissed. And some other things in my pocket, Harry. Jewels. I promised Mutti. He can't have them.

The man was nearly on us, just a couple of yards away. Cocky, self-assured, all the time in the world—and enjoying the fact!

If you give me enough, he sneered, perhaps I'll let you go. Perhaps Old Jimmy won't keep you down here for good.

Something snapped in me. I launched myself at him, so hard, so fast, that he didn't have time to react—not quickly enough anyway. I pushed him back hard against the tunnel wall, screaming at him to leave Agatha alone, grappling blindly for I don't know what—the gun or his throat maybe—and the gun went off. Thunderous in the confined space, but I just kept going, had him by the scruff of the collar. In that moment I wanted to thump him, kick him, hurt him badly. But that voice in me whispered not to, that it wouldn't relieve anything, so instead I just wanted to get him away from us both, and in a kind of weird, frantic waltz, both of us wrestling for each other, I spun him round and round, and then sent him spinning off balance along the rain-soaked passage. Falling, cursing.

Then we ran. I heard him shouting, furious, and another two shots exploded behind us. Agatha pushed through the black door, and we slammed it shut and slid two big bolts home, and slumped to the ground.

The man banged on the door. Shouted threats about what Old Jimmy would do when he finds us, *stuff you don't want to think about.* That we would *never see the light of day.* Then the thud of bullets as he emptied his gun impotently at this heavy metal door, and then silence.

And here we are.

Some kind of—what? A deep storage space? A bunker of some kind? It's big, like a cavern, but all straight lines and metal. Maybe this is where the government is planning to hide if the Germans ever get going with anything worse than V–2s: sonic rays, robots, who knows what? Low-level lighting, so dim you can feel your eyes straining, trying to make sense of it all. Pipes, walkways, wires, corridors leading off in different directions. And the hum. The hum is much louder here. You can feel it throbbing all around. God knows where we are now, but A looks calm again. She's twiddling the gold ring on her finger. Smiling a thin smile, whispering to herself, lost in something I can't see. I'm sure I didn't notice that ring before. Odd.

My head's so foggy.

Everything's slipping.

———————

The Ring

It was a last-minute thing

— the giving of the ring.

When,

in the moment before the train departed,

Agatha's mother, who knew she must not cry,

slid the ring from her fumbling fingers

and reached towards her daughter.

From the platform below

it was nearly too far,

but Agatha

leaned

out.

Mother and daughter:

their fingers brushed

as the train huffed and hushed,

and jolted to life.

And Agatha's mother thought, Remember me!

Dear child, remember me!

For this is the end of our time together;

this is the end

of our time.

Agatha gripped the ring

and stared as her mother grew smaller and smaller,

until she was lost from sight.

Then, as London grew bigger and bigger,

Agatha stared at the ring,

that symbol of love, eternal and right.

And placed on her finger,

there the ring stayed,

day, after day, after London day

as Agatha tried to make herself thin,

the better to blend with the people of London,

the people who'd taken her in.

Agatha did what her mother had told her

the moment she stepped from the rescuing train.

She never spoke German,

and she never complained.

She spoke when supposed to;

she always said please,

and slowly she started

to feel more at ease.

She played with children,

she even laughed, and tried

very hard not to think of the past.

Agatha.

She might have become someone,

someone strong.

She would have grown up

knowing right from wrong.

She could have been famous,

loved and adored;

a dancer, a singer,

who'd come from abroad.

Or maybe an intellect

so wise, so sage,

dispensing significant thoughts for our age.

She might have tried politics

and caused quite a stir

working hard to prevent

what had happened to her.

But none of this happened,

and it's all I can do

to finish the story,

to see it through.
To tell how it was
that vicious day
when fate found Agatha
and took her away.
The bomb that killed her
killed a hundred more
running to a shelter —
just short of the door
when the bomb fell,
smack!
And sent her to Hell.
Obliterated,
annihilated,
and, as if it were planned,
all that was left was that golden band,
there in the dust, a pitiful sight.
Yet perfect, eternal, and somehow right.

It was a last-minute thing
— that giving of the ring.

———————————

Later

Agatha looked up at me, pain and a kind of elation on her face at the same time. Something overwhelming. Wish I could have drawn what I saw there, but it's beyond me now.

I felt myself starting to cry—not from sadness or worry, but more like you do from relief.

Agatha leaned near and said, I think we are really close now, Harry.

I asked her if she meant to Ellis.

And she said calmly, To Ellis. To my parents. We are close to everything, Harry. Everything. We're nearly there.

Shivers right through me. It sounded so final.

I told her I didn't understand, and she looked at me and held up the ring and the jewels in the flashlight beam.

My parents are dead, Harry. They died on the way here, or before they even got out of Berlin. It was hard to explain to you before. But now you have brought me very near to them.

Poor girl. Maybe she's lost her grip on reality too. I gave her a hug, and she told me she was OK and that it was time to go.

But which way in this labyrinth? Just have to guess.

———————————

Pomegranate Seeds

_____

The beginning
to the end
has come so fast.

Every day
took us closer
to this: our last.

On this,
the final day of our existence,
it seems only right to remember
how once we were free.
Once, and not that long ago,
we walked through forests of winding innocence.
Deer darted across sunlit glades and we
	bathed our feet in streams.
In the high mountains, in summer,
the grasshoppers clicked and snakes
	cooled themselves under rocks.
Birds whirled through the lifting air;
we watched them with wonder.

We supped on honey from the comb,

drank milk from the goats;

slept by the fire, under the stars,

and knew that we were free.

We were gods, all of us,

man, and woman, and child.

Every day we made our own;

every day was a seed,

easily sown.

On this, the final day of our existence,

it would satisfy me if you would merely look at what we've made.

How we cut down those forests, eagerly!

How we shut out the night!

How we made our cities of electric light.

Skyscrapers, roads, and underground trains,

car parks and shopping streets,

cinemas of electric fantasy,

dance halls and theaters,

town halls and office blocks;

and no, I do not object to the libraries,

but they are merely repositories of books that are the ghosts

of the remembrance of what we once were:

gods.

But were there days when men were gods?

Were we free?

Did we wander?

I remember a little of my boyhood days

in the mountains of Thrace.

Winter and wild horses, that's what I remember now.

Winter and wild white horses;

is it not the case that we were freer then?

Maybe I'm suffering:

a dreaded disease, a sickness with no cure;

known by the name: *nostalgia*.

A longing for what once was.

But perhaps this is a fantasy of my own;

a memory of how I would like it to be,

but *never* was.

Have we always and ever just been waiting for today?

The hum is growing louder.

As the centuries have revolved,

attempts have been made to analyze my name.

What does it mean: *Orpheus*?

Who are you? What can your name tell us about *you*?

Beautiful of voice, some would have it,

yet there are other ideas,

and this is the one that I know best:

Orpheus, orphne, ορφνη;

the darkness of the night.

For that is where we are heading now: darkness.

Nostalgia? A good Greek word.

(We had a word for everything.)

Nostos, homecoming. The womb.

We wish to return to whence we came,

and whence we came was . . . darkness.

To darkness we shall return.

And here for Harry, and Agatha, darkness is already present:

and all the horrors of the Underworld.

She trembles as she follows Harry down,

hand in hand, step-by-step.

Revulsion and terror lie at the wayside;

shapes half seen by twilight,

hints of everlasting pain,

torture and torment,

figures writhing in the eternal dusk of Hell.

Agatha, you don't need to be afraid.

That time is gone for you;

and you know, you're right;

the end is in sight.

Agatha, *anima*, little girl,

you are much misunderstood.

Meek (what a denigrated word!).

Peaceful, kind, gentle, wise:

there's a touch of you in all of us,

if only we'd let it be.

If only we'd give it room to live,

space to breathe, a chance to grow.

If only we thought more of you.

Raised you up and worshipped you,

drew a circle of protection about you;

but it seems that you're not valued anymore;

not as much as money and war.

Agatha,

my tale is very old,

but so, I think, is yours.

Emigrant, exile.

Refugee and railway truck,

or you trudge across the world

a pack on your back;

bent against the weight

of the fear as much as the enemy drawing near.

Agatha,

they tell of the tale of Ajax,

Odysseus and more;

how Paris's love for Helen

led to epic war.

Achilles slaughtered Hector, dragged his body through the dust.

They sing of deeds so brutal,

give them glory, give them fame,

but where is the song for Agatha?

Where do they sing her name?

No one sings for Agatha,

the refugee of war;

no one sings of misery

or the disregarded poor.

Refugees, in the cold;

at the border,

at the gate,

trapped behind the barbed-wire fence,

abandoned to fate.

O Agatha!

I'll sing for you!

I'll defend you to the last.

I'll sing and sing; I'll tell your tale.

Your story; *my* final task.

I'll paint a portrait,

write a play,

make everybody know someday

your story must be heard.

And though I must tell everyone,

I know that many will not hear;

they do not want to listen to such tales

of unexciting fear.

But trust me, Agatha;

come what may

I'll sing your story anyway.

I have no doubt,

I do not tire,

my song will be eternal fire,

and,

if just one person understands

why you're important,

why the past
must teach us something,
then I'll know
this story had a point at last.

But the hum is getting louder.

A lady sits in the shade, eating seeds from a ripened pomegranate.
She plucks each red jewel,
slips it between her withering lips,
and though only honey is sweeter,
to her, each seed tastes bitter.
A lady sits in the shade.
Her head lifts,
her eyes fix.
Her lips smile,
but only her lips.
She seems to see only Agatha,
and now she stands
and approaches,
her skin as white as my gypsum was.
Once elegant, now decaying,
a hint of her beauty yet remains.

A glimmer of sunshine clings to her,

the sunlight of only half a year.

Behind, on her table:

wilting flowers and rotting fruit.

Behind that, an open door,

from where the hum is louder still.

And where a towering figure

can just be seen,

hunched over a desk that glows with a somehow fearsome light.

He gets up from his chair, steps out of his lair.

Turns a threatening gaze on Harry and the girl.

Then the lady whispers into his ear,

he frowns,

she waves a hand,

they talk,

he turns around

and goes back to his cave,

grunting in satisfaction.

No more talk of him, not yet.

Closer the lady comes,

draped in robes of flowing white,

glowing despite the feeble light.

Her hand is before her; she speaks her name.

I remember this moment all too well;

I see that Harry catches his breath

as he sees

Persephone,

she who causes death.

Agatha seems unafraid.

She lets Harry's hand slip from hers,

and why?

She has seen something in Persephone,

some story that is like her own:

raped,

and ripped from her earthly home,

dragged against her will to this Underworld,

to rule in darkness; and to aid

Hades, Lord of Shade.

Persephone lights upon the girl,

takes a pallid hand with hers;

and Agatha says, Persephone,

you look a little bit like me.

Harry's seen it too.

And now he sees something else:

in the dark, at the far end of a tunnel.

Two figures emerge, no more than shapes:

a man and a woman,

standing and watching and waiting.

Persephone lifts a once-fair hand

and turns Agatha's head. Turns her gaze to the tunnel,

to where the woman is waving.

Mutti!

cries Agatha.

Mother!

Then, Father! Are you there too?

Bist du *schon da?*

And Agatha runs.

They wait,

then fold her into themselves

and disappear.

On this, the final day of our existence,

it would gratify me if you would do just one thing.

If you would only ask yourself: Why are we here?

Why did we come?

Why did we venture away from the sun?

I only have answers of my own,

which you might not like,

or even want to know.

But this is what we hoped for,

and why we came:

regeneration through downward motion

(it's darkest just before the dawn),

recognition through remembrance,

and, with luck, the attendant self-transformation.

But Agatha's death undoes it all.

Agatha, it seemed you'd lost your parents;

they thought they'd lost you too.

You found them again in this Underworld,

mysterious, perhaps. But true.

And now I only ask one thing

as you start your life anew.

Do you think *anyone* understands

what we lose when we lose you?

———————————

1st Jan.?, Sewer tunnel

I have so many questions. And no way of answering them, it seems.

For starters: *Who* am I?

Feels like there was a glue that held all the pieces of me together, and now it's coming unstuck and the pieces are going to fly apart and disappear. Or become someone else? Maybe that doesn't matter.

Secondly: *Where* am I?

I remember what Agatha said to me back in the Royal Free. *You go right and left and then straight on. And then there is no more direction anymore.* Feels like that now—there is no more direction. But still somehow I have to keep going, find Ellis, before those bits of me are scattered.

So tired now, but I need to set down what just happened. Thought this journal would help me create *Warriors of the Machine*. Now it's simply a matter of survival. For me, for someone, for no one.

Short-term memory feels like a broken mirror. Just bright bits and pieces.

How I recall it: First, the woman; then, behind her, the tramp, Old Jimmy, sitting in his wing-backed, beaten-up old chair like some kind of beggar king, shotgun casually pointed at us. A thousand-yard stare that seemed to see right through me. The woman standing next to him in the shadows, dark hair and pale face, half a smile, some kind of fruit in her hand. And overhead, dim but constant, constant, constant, the rumble of strikes from V-1s and V-2s raining down on the city. The sound of 1945.

Old Jimmy got slowly to his feet, cleared his throat, eyes sharp in that battered ancient face. Said nothing for a minute or more but just stared at us.

Then, his voice deep, broken: How did you find me?

I told him we were lost, and he laughed. Aren't we all?

We're looking for someone, I said. My brother. I think he's down here somewhere.

He shook his head. No one alive down here but me and my lovely Cora.

The woman behind him smiled and took a bite of some weird fruit. Fruit! Where the hell did she get that, I thought.

And I rule these tunnels, the man added. This is my domain, and I'm keeping it to myself. No one must know I'm down here. I don't want people telling them up there about me. Can't let you go.

The woman leaned forward and whispered in his ear then. They seemed to argue, almost without words.

He shook his head, raised the gun, fingers tightening—but the dark-haired woman kept whispering to him, more urgently now. I held A tight, braced.

An enormous impact overhead shook the walls around us, and for a moment I thought he'd fired.

War's not been bad for me, he growled. I control more than I used to. Don't want any witnesses to that.

Then a blank.

Next I remember Jimmy laughing. Expression changed utterly.

Cora says if you pay me some tribute, I'm to let you go. She says you'll know to keep silent. But I need something special. I've no need for money or coupons or chocolate. We've got fruit, as you see. Give me something I haven't seen before; give me something bee-yoo-ti-ful. As beautiful as that tune.

Couldn't understand what he meant, but now I heard Agatha's voice. Calm, clear. Give him the rest of the eyes, Harry, she said. It's time.

The man looked interested at that. Eyes? What eyes? he growled.

I reached slowly into my pocket, grabbed all

the eyeballs but one, five of them, felt their cool glass, felt reluctant—terribly reluctant—to give them but knew I had to. (Feels somehow like when the eyes are gone, I'll be gone. But still I have one left.)

Old Jimmy took them, weighed them in his big, scarred palm. And then smiled, a huge beam of a smile.

No one ever gave me eyes before, lad. What a blue. A bloody midsummer morning! Larks singing above you, that kind of thing! Gentle breezes . . .

He put the gun down, leaned it against his knackered old chair.

I *know* where your brother is.

He waved a hand over his shoulder at the gloom. One of my lads saw someone, down an old sewer. That way. Still alive yesterday. Not a nice crawl though. Dangerous. Not nice for your young lady.

My heart leaped. Where? I shouted. Just show me where.

And now the woman spoke, a quiet voice, just audible over that persistent humming, the impact of bombs overhead.

I'll look after the girl for you, she said.

And now the fog comes down in my head again. Just bits and pieces. The woman drew nearer and said, or I imagined she said, You have kept your promise. Her parents are close.

And Agatha said, It is all OK, Harry. *Danke sehr.* I am going now. You kept your promise.

I felt her kiss my cheek.

And then she walked down a corridor to my left. There was smoke or dust sifting down from the new wave of rockets overhead. Light, bright and streaming through it from somewhere. Ground shaking.

I wanted to follow but couldn't move. As if in a dream, I watched Agatha walking away with that tall, dark woman, thin and pale by her side, fading in the dust.

And then, for a brief second, I saw them: a young couple, faint, like a projection in a room that's too bright, the man's arm around the woman's shoulder, and her white dress blowing in a breeze. Just as in the photograph. Agatha ran towards them, and they opened their arms to her—and they all disappeared.

And I cried.

Passed out, I think. No idea how long.

Clearly I'm cracked.

Broken.

And too tired to write more.

———————

Warriors of the Machine

If I, Orpheus, have a thousand names,
then Hades has a thousand more.
Hades, Lord Shade, Lord of the Underworld,
ruler of the land of the dead.
Irkalla, Osiris, Thanatos, Hel,
Satan, Lucifer, Beelzebub.
Pluto. Baron Samedi.
Batara Kala,
Kalma, Kali, Mot.
Or, as Harry would have it, Old Jimmy.

His story is even older than mine.
Many believe him evil,
but of that I cannot say,
I only know that when I came before him,
my skin painted white,
my lyre in my hand and a song on my lips,
I had him stand still.
Stopped him from speaking.
I, Orpheus, charmed Death himself,

and, for a moment, made him weep.

I sang not so much of Eurydice;

I sang of the world above.

I sang of the light that comes with dawn,

of rose-red sunshine piercing the mist.

Of how the birds begin to sing

when sunlight breaks the night.

I sang of the dew on the mountainside,

of salmon in the river;

of apples falling from the bough,

of the silver light of winter.

I sang of the touch of gentlest breeze,

of the beat of goose on the wing;

I sang of wine,

and other things equally divine.

I sang not so much of Eurydice, but of what she'd left

    behind, and when my song was over, I opened my

    eyes and found Eurydice standing there; and then

    Hades spoke the only words I needed him to.

Go, he said. Go, and don't look back.

Lead her from this place, and don't look

    back until you are both safe away.

We fled.

Hades-Jimmy in his lair,

sits upon a terrible chair; a throne of bone.

A seat composed of the souls he's sifted;

those he's taken away.

Before Jimmy, Harry sees some kind of table,

a vast and ranging desk,

with lights and dials and knobs and switches;

and things like television screens,

glowing green.

It is from this desk that the humming comes.

That appalling hum, like the sound of the Earth shaking,

like the Earth is quaking from insentient fear.

Jimmy? says Harry, drawing near;

but the Lord of the Dead seems not to hear.

All his attention is trained on the desk,

which he scrutinizes, incessantly.

His eyes are fixed upon a screen

that speaks a language Harry doesn't know.

Then Harry sees Hades' hand hovering,

above a certain switch, a button,

over which his finger trembles; hesitating.

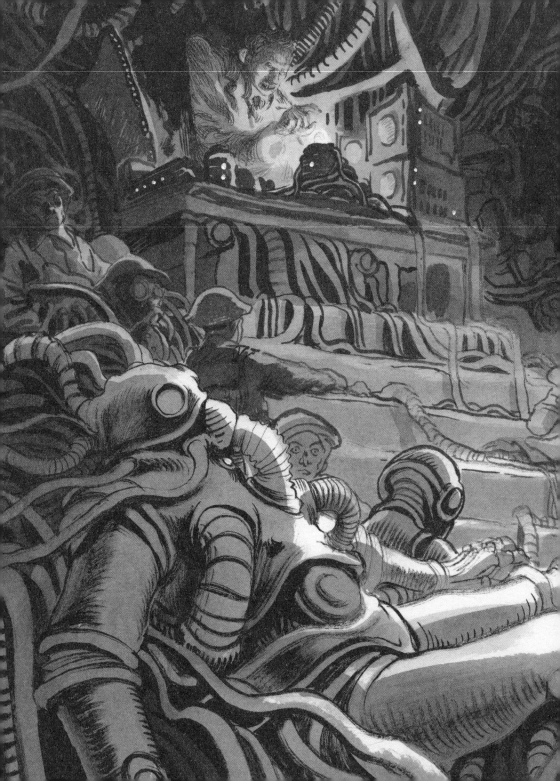

The humming sound is too much to bear.

Harry shoves his hands to his head.

Jimmy! he shouts. What *is* this machine?

What does it mean?

He shouts twice, and twice more,

and now Hades appears to hear;

turns his face to Harry.

This? he says. *This?*

This is the ultimate machine of war;

this is what it's all been for.

All the killing, all the bleeding,

this is where it's all been leading.

The rock, the club, the knife of stone:

as clumsy as that hefted bone.

Artless, they seemed, simplistic, and yet

you had no idea then, I'll bet,

of where they'd lead,

but this is it:

the very end of everything.

Hades explains to Harry just what he's looking at.

    The cleverest machine of war,

the cleverest machine by far. Such an idea! What killing conceit!

To make a machine to manage the fighting; give control
of warfare to machines themselves.

It is not activated.
But all Hades has to do is depress that switch,
lower his forefinger and it will come to life,
take control of the war machines,
use them and guide them,
deploy them at will.
Man himself will no longer kill.
It will all be done by this final machine,
this very   final   machine.

Harry stares, as do I,
as the Lord of the Dead hesitates.
As even Hades,
who has welcomed the dead to his domain for eons,
hesitates.
As Hades,
for whom death itself is life,
hesitates.
And as Hades hesitates, his finger hovering,
he whispers something that's hard to hear,

so Harry steps closer, and cups his ear

to catch the thoughts in Hades' head.

Once I press the switch,

once I start the attack,

well, then, my boy,

there's no way back.

When I visited Hades, I charmed him with my

    song, but Harry's got things of different worth.

    He begs Hades for information; and after all, this

    Lord of the Underworld is well connected.

I gasp as Harry offers his tribute of five glass eyes,

five blue glass eyes; and Hades, for a moment, smiles.

That way, he says. Go. But don't look back.

Harry scrambles away down the tunnel.

Hades hesitates still, his finger hovering

above the switch of this doomsday machine.

The hum rumbles on, far underground,

a genuinely disturbing sound.

If you listen carefully, some might say

you can hear it still,

now, today.

[untitled journal entry]

Ellis.

I remember.

The dance in Knighton. When the girl I loved with the dimpled cheek (*that's* who that nurse Eunice reminded me of!) succumbed to E's charm (uniform?) rather than mine. Watched her kiss him hard under the blossoms outside the hall. I was glad for him; jealous as anything. An idiot.

I remember:

How that year and a half between us seemed to grow into more. How he took the role of adult to my lingering childishness. Started to act and talk like Father. Him the responsible one, me the prodigal. We tell the stories so we end up playing the parts. Trapped in the bloody *drama* of it all. Forgetting how just to *be*.

I remember:

My stupidity. The daft things I said to him. My stubbornness.

But I also remember when we delighted in each other's talents.

I remember the hill walks and stream charming. The days when we made up stories—weird, mad adventures—and it felt like the sparrows in the garden flew rings around us.

The joy and fights and wild games of springtime.

I remember being together.

Old Jimmy woke me and gave me some food, a dram of gin. Hurricane lamp. Showed me the way into this ancient sewer or whatever it is, and I started to crawl.

Exhausted now. Soaked through.

Writing with this blunt pencil by the last bit of flashlight beam. Been crawling for ages. Have to keep going if there's *any* chance Ellis is alive.

Sound of water ahead. Keep going.

Where *am* I going?

Where the hell are we going?

Memory: A couple of months ago—firefighting near Archway. Top of a ladder, all hell breaking loose around me, the hose kicking in my hands like a writhing python as the pressure came and went and came again. People have been known to be whisked six feet sideways off a ladder. So: focusing on my task, working out the collapse zone, flashpoints—and then suddenly no water at all. The air full of AAA and tracer, the blimps, a hundred fires burning, it seemed, across the city.

And then I saw it. Bright in a searchlight, a V-2 hurtling down. My blink freezing it perfectly in the dark air. A split second to impact, then, trailing it, the sonic boom and roar of the engine. Unbelievable what we are doing. Beyond belief. If I live through this, I shall have to work as hard as I can to create *Warriors of the Machine;* have to try and add my voice.

My voice?

Too late . . . ?

Been going ages. The sound of the water loud now, deafening. Still the occasional impact overhead. How deep am I?

Hope this journal survives if I don't.

Feel light, though. As if all the effort is leaving me. Feel like I could do anything. No me and no you. Just a bond.

Love.

Last eyeball is for Ellis.

A kind of subterranean river flowing past me. A few yards beyond, it drops into a pit. God knows how deep. Thunderous roar from the depths. And across the falling water I can see a ruined underground space: debris, beams, rubble, bright light, so bright, streaming down. Like sunlight. Morning light.

I think I can
see a way across.
Someone lying
there.

Transformation

_____

When you follow a path to find yourself,

mistakes are inevitable.

That's another thing I've learned

as the years have cycled;

another thing I didn't know when I first set foot in Hell.

Eurydice.

The story of my love for her is without equal;

a tale of great fame.

But just as great is the fame of my mistake.

She followed me back out of Hell,

past Tantalus and Sisyphus,

and Cerberus, that drooling beast,

across the Styx in Charon's boat,

heading back towards the light.

I reached the mouth of the cave,

felt sunshine on my face,

and . . .

I turned.

I looked.

She looked back at me, still in the realm of the dark.

She had not yet left Hell.

Now she would never leave.

That is the story of my mistake;

and so very many people know it.

But they don't know the look that was upon her face

as she faded.

What do you think it was?

Anger?

No.

Recrimination? Fear?

No.

Betrayal, sadness, or perhaps loss?

No.

Acceptance mixed with understanding,

that's what it was.

A slight smile.

She understood.

For her, she'd begun to live in the land of the dead.

Too late now to return to the light.

Too bright now, too much joy;

time instead to learn what *decaying* means.

For me, she knew something that I did not yet know:

something it would take me *years* to learn.

They call me *psychopomp*, a guider of souls,

but it was Eurydice who guided *me* first.

Who was she really?

Why did she go?

Why did she lead me below?

As she drifted back,

that hint of a smile on her face,

so enigmatic.

It took me years to realize what she already knew:

I did not go after death to find her;

I went after *her* to find *death*.

That is my story, my *true* story.

Even greater than my story of love:

my search for the understanding of death.

So when I lost her, that second time,

standing in the mouth of the cave.

Well, it was no failure,

no mistake.

It was simply what had to be,

as Eurydice continued a process,

that led me, in time, to me.

As Eurydice, so Agatha,

who has now performed mystical transformation upon Harry.

Here in the deepest bowel of London's underbelly,

this is not a place of wonder and fame;

this is a place of forgotten emotions

that no one wants to glorify.

No warriors here,

no heroes;

just Harry crawling with his brother on his back.

———————————

Transformation 2

These are the final words of my song.
It didn't take long
to tell you of Harry, Orpheus Black,
who crawled into Hell,
and returned.
His brother on his back.

Step by weary step Harry came; carrying Ellis in a
    fireman's lift; and yet it was not the brother he knew
    from six days before. Ellis had lain in darkness
    for six days: no food, dripping water all there was
    to drink, till he had passed from consciousness,
    passed from this world so nearly to the next.

There was plenty of time for him to think,
plenty of time for him to dream;
so now, as he's hoisted on Harry's back,
things are not, perhaps, what they seem.
Transformation occurring,
love redeeming,
understanding flows from one to the other;

and Ellis begins to understand
how he's misunderstood his brother.

Harry takes almost half a day
to bring Ellis back to the light.

Along the way, transformation occurs.
As Ellis lay in the dark,
there was plenty of time for me to whisper into his ear:
stop, Ellis; listen, Ellis;
understand your brother!
Remember who you truly are;
live your own life, and no other.

So Ellis is reborn, from darkness.
So Harry feels his load lighten as they approach the surface.
So the gap between them closes.

Harry sets Ellis on the broken ground,
lies down beside him.
I close my eyes,
my inner gaze moves from brother to brother,
and as Harry finally slips away, I know
it's time for me to go, to help another.

It's time for me to sing my song

to someone else's ear;

time to share the gifts I've gained

as musician, poet, seer.

The journey has been dark at times,

I can't deny the pain,

the broken shells of understanding

you lose so you may gain.

And people think I went alone,

when I journeyed underground;

that I made my way unaided

as I ventured deeper down.

In fact, the very opposite

would be closer to the truth,

for at my heels came a crowd

of people seeking proof.

Writers, poets, philosophers,

some timid and some brave,

makers of moving images,

musicians both wild and grave.

Painters by the score there were,

artists with sight and sound;

a giant host of pilgrims

came to witness what I found.
And what was that, what did I find,
when I ventured into Hell?
A little bit about death, of course,
but a lot about life, as well.

So.
Now.
It's time.
We're done, and
along with all the talk of death,
the anguish, and the shuddered breath,
were words of understanding too
which may transform you into you.
So when at last my journey's done,
and I absent myself from strife,
I hope you know what I know now:
my song was not of death,
but life.

———————————

You may already have guessed that I am Orpheus. By which I mean
that I am responsible for the poetry in this book, and any merit or
deficiency it may have. Where I have succeeded in helping my brother
to tell the story he wanted to tell I am pleased. Some of his drawings
for that project have survived; others have been created from the
words in his journal. In places I have tidied or enhanced those words
themselves — and added a few where I was sure I could speak those words
for him — to help make sense of the tangle of his thoughts. Shaping a
few things where maybe he would have said more had he had the time.

The doctors at the Royal Free told me it was a miracle he kept going as
long as he did. And of young Agatha I could find no record at all . . .

It's taken me far, far longer than I would have liked to produce this
book. It was hard to write. And as it isn't the work Harry envisaged, but a
product of both of our efforts, I have decided to give the work a new title:
Voyages in the Underworld of Orpheus Black.

Ellis Black
Berlin, 1984

The Mansion by the Geran Sea
Shingle Street,
Woodbridge,
Suffolk

January 6, 1946

Father,

Thank you for your letters. I got some in Germany;
the rest were waiting when I arrived home to get
demobilized. I was lucky: my turn came quickly.
Demobbing's a funny business. It's an anticlimax, let
me tell you. You sign, they sign, and then you're no
longer Lieutenant Ellis Black, you're just Ellis from
the Marches, and you get a train to London staring at
everything, wondering how life is still going on.

I apologize for not writing sooner. I've been
wandering. Do you know where I went? Germany.
Something drew me back again.

By the way, don't think from my address that I'm
living the high life. The name of the cottage is
<u>heavily</u> ironic. After wandering through Germany, I
drifted home again, and somehow ended up here, in
Suffolk. Shingle Street is a single row of cottages,
right on the beach. I'm renting one for a while: the

Mansion is two tiny semi-detached cottages. Inland you can see the Suffolk marshes; looking out the other way, as I am now, you can see across the water. When the wind blows, you think it's going to pick the house up and whisk it over the sea, drop it into Europe. You can't see it, of course, but you can feel Belgium right there, and Germany beyond.

Germany again. How long will it take us to unpick the mess we've made? That's why I had to go back, to see what we'd done to Mutti's homeland, and I assure you, we made a bigger mess of German cities than they made of British ones. I know you don't want to hear this, Father, but it's true. The weapons your factory makes did it. And yes, the Germans outdid us with their rocket bombs, but we would have done just the same to them if we'd been smart enough to build something like that.

Germany. You've probably seen the newsreels: about the camps, I mean. A sanitized snippet of horror that cannot be put into words and which I refuse to write about here. It is enough to know that having seen the things I saw last April in Nordhausen, well, you cannot look at the world the same way again.

And you will say, "There you are, Ellis, that is why you were fighting: you were fighting against this evil; that is what justifies our guns and bombs and the killing and the firestorms." But I say this to you: I know now that the opposite is true. We cannot go on answering hate with hate, because it's only when we answer it with understanding that things will change. And that's why Harry was right.

You won't know that I saw Harry, one last time. You won't know that it was Harry who saved me in London. He tunneled into the ground, into the broken Earth, and carried me back up to the surface. Harry. Your cowardly son. He faced death to save me and then death got the better of him.

He believed our true enemies are not other peoples across seas and on far continents; our true enemies are <u>ourselves</u>: our fears, our prejudices. We must, each of us, rise up and overthrow the tyranny found inside that keeps us fearing what we do not know, because from that fear comes hate. That is our true enemy: our lack of understanding; not only of other people, but of ourselves.

And that's why Harry was right, because the best way to learn about ourselves is through words, through imagination. He wanted to draw what he was seeing around him so he could hold those pictures up and say, Look! Why? What is this for? And I shouldn't have been fighting; I should have been writing: to make something valuable, something that matters.

Harry had an idea for a book. An important book.

I have his sketches, his notes and drawings. I can see what he was seeing in London as he worked to save people from the fires and the rubble. His book was to be called <u>Warriors of the Machine</u>, and I am going to take what he had so far and make something with it.

I shall take Harry's diary, and where there are blanks, I will write some words of my own. I'll write

for both of us now; I will <u>be</u> Harry. I'll tell the
story of how we went into the Underworld and faced
death, and how one of us survived and the other died.

Though he's dead and I live, in the book we will
both live forever. And both be dead forever too, I
suppose, but that's one thing I've learned. Through
the war, through Harry, through my wanderings,
through Orpheus—being alive and being dead are
twins, two sides of a coin, you might say. We cannot
know one without the other; and in some way that I
cannot yet put into words, we are all both alive and
dead <u>at the same time</u>: each state exists inside the
other, and in that way, we are <u>all</u> Orpheus if we want
to be.

If we want to be.

Father, I don't know if we shall see each other
again. I know how painful it was for you when Mutti
died. You disowned Harry, but I hope now you will
forgive him. And if—when—we do meet again, either
in this world or in the one under our feet, I will
greet you with love, and hope only that you can do
the same for me. And for Harry.

Yours,

Well, the first War of the Machines seems
to be drawing to its final inconclusive
chapter—leaving, alas, everyone the poorer,
many bereaved or maimed and millions dead,
and only one thing triumphant: the Machines.

J.R.R. Tolkien in a letter to his son, 1945

*Our thanks as ever to our families, whose love and support
makes writing possible. At Walker Books we are grateful
for the enthusiasm and attention to detail of Lizzie Sitton,
Gill Evans, Maria Soler Canton, and Ben Norland.
And, of course, heartfelt thanks to Alexis Deacon
for bringing Harry's vision so wonderfully to life.*

*Unlike the father of the brothers in this book, our father was
a Quaker and conscientious objector. His registration card
and tribunal letter are the basis for Harry's documents . . .*

M. S. & J. S.

Text copyright © 2019 by Julian Sedgwick and Marcus Sedgwick
Illustrations copyright © 2019 by Alexis Deacon

All rights reserved. No part of this book may be reproduced, transmitted, or stored
in an information retrieval system in any form or by any means, graphic, electronic,
or mechanical, including photocopying, taping, and recording, without prior written
permission from the publisher.

First U.S. edition 2019

Library of Congress Catalog Card Number pending
ISBN 978-1-5362-0437-7

19 20 21 22 23 24 CCP 10 9 8 7 6 5 4 3 2 1

Printed in Shenzhen, Guangdong, China

This book was typeset in Bembo, Fell Type, and Trixie.
The illustrations were done in acrylic ink, watercolor, charcoal, and gouache.

Walker Books
a division of
Candlewick Press
99 Dover Street
Somerville, Massachusetts 02144

www.walkerbooksus.com

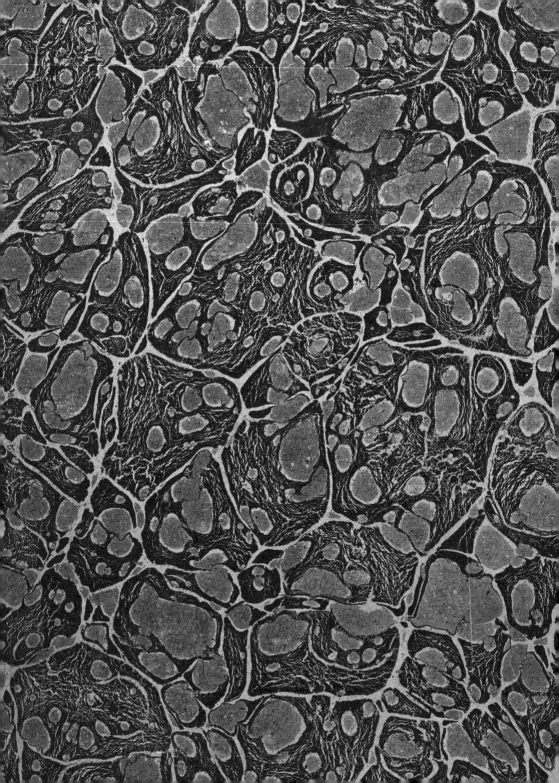